THE QUEST OF THE RECLUSIVE ROGUE

REMINGTONS OF THE REGENCY
BOOK FOUR

ELLIE ST. CLAIR

CONTENTS

Chapter 1   1

Chapter 2   8

Chapter 3   16

Chapter 4   26

Chapter 5   37

Chapter 6   45

Chapter 7   53

Chapter 8   61

Chapter 9   69

Chapter 10   77

Chapter 11   86

Chapter 12   94

Chapter 13   104

Chapter 14   111

Chapter 15   119

Chapter 16   127

Chapter 17   138

Chapter 18   147

Chapter 19   157

Chapter 20   165

Chapter 21   171

Chapter 22   178

Chapter 23   187

Chapter 24   194

Chapter 25   201

Chapter 26   208

Chapter 27   215

Epilogue   224

The Earl's Secret - Chapter One   231

Also by Ellie St. Clair   241

About the Author   245

Facebook: Ellie St. Clair

Cover by AJF Designs

Do you love historical romance? Receive access to a free ebook, as well as exclusive content such as giveaways, contests, freebies and advance notice of pre-orders through my mailing list!

Sign up here!

The Remingtons of the Regency
The Mystery of the Debonair Duke
The Secret of the Dashing Detective
The Clue of the Brilliant Bastard
The Quest of the Reclusive Rogue

For a full list of all of Ellie's books, please see
www.elliestclair.com/books.

CHAPTER 1

*P*rudence stood in the shadows at the back of the room, one hand on the hilt of her sword, ready to draw it against anyone who approached.

Not that she was in any danger at the moment. But she had become rather used to being on her guard, whether it was here on the hallowed ground of Angelo's Fencing Academy or as she traversed the streets between the school and Warwick House.

She was accustomed to the room being filled with the sounds of swords clashing and men alternately gasping or cheering, a place where she always found contentment. Of course, she couldn't completely be herself, for Lady Prudence Remington should never be caught in a fencing academy – as a viewer would be horror enough, but as a participant? She couldn't deny, however, that she was far more at home here among strangers who had no idea the truth of her identity than she was standing in the middle of a ballroom curtseying demurely at any gentleman who approached.

"Why are we requested to be here today?" she asked Hugo in a low voice. She typically joined in with the gentlemen who remained to watch the other matches, taking her turn when it was required. But Hugo had sent her a note to arrive early, as requested by fencing master Henry Angelo himself. The room felt oddly empty, despite the rapiers on the wall, and she tapped her foot impatiently as they waited for Mr. Angelo to arrive.

Usually she was filled with confidence when she entered Angelo's, her single fear that someone would discover she was not Peter Robertson. There was never a doubt in her actual ability. She was well aware that she could best whoever she faced. She had dueled most men here at Angelo's and had nearly always emerged the victor.

She just wished they all knew that they had been bested by a woman.

Had Angelo finally discovered her true identity?

"Nothing to fear," Hugo murmured. "Angelo will be here any moment. It sounds as though he has someone he wanted you to bout privately."

"But who?" she asked her friend, the only man who knew all her secrets, who understood who she was, through and through – as she did him.

"I am uncertain. Angelo said it would be a good match."

Prudence nodded as she drew a breath, centering herself, before Henry Angelo walked into the room.

"Mr. Robertson. Mr. Conway. Thank you for coming."

"Of course."

"I understand this is rather unusual, but your opponent prefers private matches."

She nodded as she stepped into the center of the room, taking on her identity as Mr. Peter Robertson. She was actually rather proud that Angelo had thought of her for a private match. It meant that she had finally made the name for herself that she had been striving for – even if the name was contrived. Any femininity of her features, of which she was

2

lacking in comparison to her sister or sister-in-law, of that she was certain, was explained by the youth she claimed. She had begun as an underdog, but no longer.

As she waited for her opponent, she tried to inhale deeply, but the linen she had wrapped tightly around her breasts restrained her movements. Then a man stepped out of the shadows where she hadn't even realized he had been lurking, and into the light in front of her.

Prudence sucked in a breath. She knew this man. Not well – no one knew him well, as far as she was aware. However, all knew of his brooding, reclusive ways.

Recently she had also become interested in learning more about him, for he very well could be the man who had killed her father.

"Mr. Peter Robertson versus Lord Trundelle," said Mr. Angelo, before taking a step back, giving them room. "If you are ready, begin."

Prudence nodded to Lord Trundelle, although his presence had sent her emotions into turmoil. What was he doing here? She had heard that he excelled in the sport, but very few had ever actually seen him fence. He was hard to read, his face as dark as his looks. His chestnut hair was a touch too long, hiding most of his forehead, though she could see his eyes were a deep brown, within strong, intimidating features. She did all she could not to prevent herself from becoming distracted.

She stood straight on her legs, her body sideways, her head upright as she looked Lord Trundelle in the eye, trying to decipher something – anything – within the depths of his face. He would be a handsome man, she considered, if he didn't always look as though he was ready to murder someone.

The thought caused a shiver to run down her spine, for there was a very good chance that he had done exactly that.

But there was nothing to be gained by contemplating such things at the moment. All she could do now was best him as she knew she was capable. Her right arm hung over her thigh; her left arm bent toward her left hip as she had been taught.

She pointed her right foot toward Lord Trundelle, and then, holding her sword near the hook of the scabbard, she lifted it out, keeping her eyes on Lord Trundelle as she bent her right arm and raised it to the height of her shoulder, making a circle over her head before lifting her left arm to the back and readying herself for whatever Lord Trundelle had to send toward her.

She was caught off-guard when he followed none of the same movements as she had, movements that she had been precisely taught. She had to resist glancing over toward Henry Angelo to see what his opinion was on Lord Trundelle's rather unorthodox greeting, but she couldn't risk taking her eyes off the man – here or anywhere else he might appear.

She narrowed her eyes, trying to determine if he knew who she was, but he showed no sign of recognition. Unless he had been watching their family – although she wouldn't put it past him – he had no reason to be aware of her identity.

Lord Trundelle simply lifted his sword from his scabbard and pointed it toward her.

He made no move but stood and stared at her. Prudence finally had enough of the game and decided to place her attack.

She thrust. He parried. She thrust again, this time from the inside to the outside of his sword, but he flicked her away as though she was an annoying insect. Again and again, she made her attempts, endeavors that worked every time against other opponents, but he seemed to guess each move she made. Finally, realizing she was needlessly tiring herself, Prudence sat back and waited for him to advance instead.

He stood, the two of them facing off against one another, neither of them moving, until her patience eventually paid off. He stepped forward, only instead of one attack, he made a series of fast movements, obviously trying to trick her. But Prudence was too quick for that. She was ready for him, countering him when he feinted inside and then attacked from the outside. His eyes flashed in some admiration, and she took that moment to turn her wrist and quickly take him off guard, the point of her sword coming to sit against his chest.

His admiration quickly turned to smouldering anger, so fierce that she almost retreated a step away, dropping her position.

When Angelo called the point, she stepped back and they began again. However, this time there was no patience, no waiting in Lord Trundelle's attack. He had obviously not appreciated being bested, even if it was just a point, which in turn heated Prudence's blood. This was a sport. It was back and forth. She had as much right to win as he did, and she was certainly going to make it so.

He would have no idea what was coming at him.

* * *

BENEDICT WAS BEING BEATEN by a fresh-faced youth.

The lad was challenging him more than any other had in some time now, though it was not often that he allowed Angelo to set up a match for him. He far preferred to practice at home or have Angelo come to him.

When the fencing master had told him about the phenomenon all were talking about, Benedict knew he had to see for himself if there was any truth to the rumors.

And he was not interested in inviting a stranger to his home.

He'd watched as the figure had stepped into the room, brimming with the same confidence that Benedict felt when he approached a match, the confidence he wished he had in the rest of his life. This Mr. Robertson was slightly on the short side, lean and wiry. Had it been any other sport, Benedict was sure that he could have bested him with one hand. But this was fencing. A sport of skill, speed, and prowess, so it was impossible to count anyone out based on appearance alone.

Benedict, however, possessed more skill, speed, and prowess than most others, so he didn't think he would have any issue. He had been wrong.

Robertson had obviously been taught by Angelo, or a pupil of his, for he used all his techniques to begin the match. Where Benedict had thought he would continue to be predictable, however, the man had surprised him, seemingly understanding each of Benedict's next moves. He had a grace and ease of movement that reminded Benedict of a dance, and the more he parried and attacked, the more Benedict had the feeling that something about this man wasn't right.

He couldn't have said why the niggling doubt was taunting him, for it made so little sense even to him that he could not properly explain it.

Benedict pushed aside the thought as Robertson waited for him to attack again, but this time Benedict held back. He was always at his best when he could wait and parry, and then when his opponent tired, make his move to defeat him.

Robertson, however, kept himself so closed off and was of such slighter build than Benedict that it made it difficult to find a point for his blade.

Until finally – there. He extended his sword within and nicked the man's shoulder, accidentally causing a tear in the fabric of his shirt right beside where his vest covered him. The man jumped back in alarm, bringing a hand to his shoulder as though his flesh had been nicked by the blade, even though Benedict knew that was an impossibility.

Angelo called a halt in play.

"Robertson? Is all well?"

"Yes," Robertson said in a grunt as his friend leaned forward in his seat as though he was about to jump up and protect him. "But I—I must forfeit."

"Forfeit?" Angelo cried, his expression darkening. "Surely not. Not if you are uninjured. You are near to winning."

"No," Benedict agreed firmly. "You cannot. We are not done here."

For even if Robertson would technically lose by forfeiting the match, Benedict would be well aware that he had won merely by default. Which did not sit well with him. Not at all. He had to win, and he had to win by his own merit.

"I must," Robertson said in a voice slightly more panicked and high-pitched as he backed away, still holding up his shirt material on his shoulder, which made no sense at all to Benedict. "A rematch, perhaps?"

"No," Benedict said again, more firmly this time. "We will finish this."

"I must go," Robertson with a desperate glance toward the man who had sat watching them. He immediately jumped up and nodded.

"Apologies, Lord Trundelle. Angelo. We shall see you again."

Angelo crossed his arms over his chest, seeming as dismayed as Benedict at the interruption of the match.

"I won't forget this, Robertson," he said, shaking his head.

"I understand," was all the youth said before nearly fleeing from the room, leaving Benedict and Angelo staring after him in dismay and incredulity.

CHAPTER 2

*P*rudence wasn't sure if she was embarrassed or annoyed. She had been winning the match – she knew she was – and was proud of it.

Then damn Lord Trundelle had to rip her shirt and threaten to expose her and her secret. She knew the chance of her linen wrap being displayed was low, but she couldn't risk the possibility. For even that small chance was enough to ruin everything she had worked so hard for.

She shivered as she recalled the way Lord Trundelle had stared at her, with such disdain in his eyes. They were hard, unrelenting, and she had no problem believing everything that anyone had ever said about him – and everything that she believed him to have done.

"It was really not that bad," Hugo said, huffing slightly as he worked hard to keep up with her. They were of similar height, Prudence being rather on the tall side for a woman, but she worked more on her stamina than most men did. In fact, if a gentleman were ever to see her without her gown – not that it was ever likely – she was sure they would be disgusted by her lack of womanly curves.

"I know, and perhaps I am being a fool," she said, shaking her head. "But he came too close."

Hugo eyed her with interest. "Would you have been so concerned had he been anyone else, or was it *because* he was Lord Trundelle that you are so upset about his actions?"

Prudence paused for a moment before answering truthfully – as she always did for Hugo – "A bit of both, perhaps."

They turned a corner and took the back stairs of the boarding house to Hugo's rooms. She always stopped here to change her clothing in between Angelo's and Warwick House. Here she would don a day dress over her fencing clothes, as she certainly couldn't leave the house in the tight breeches and shirt she wore to fence.

"You would have won, you know," Hugo said through the wall that separated him from his bedroom where Prudence was changing, the rumble of his voice vibrating through the timber between them.

"I know," she said somewhat desperately. "If only I had stepped back. Or if it had happened a few minutes later. I would have scored enough points. I know I would have."

"If only," he murmured. "But we cannot change what has happened." He paused. "Lord Trundelle is a more skilled fencer than I realized."

"He is," she agreed, emerging from the bedroom and turning so that Hugo could help with the buttons of her dress. "I wonder how his skill came to be, considering that hardly anyone has ever seen him fence."

"I have heard that Angelo offers him private lessons."

"Interesting," she murmured as she began to untie the queue she always placed her hair in as Peter before running her fingers through it and then pinning it back atop her head. Hugo lifted one of his thick brows as he watched her.

"I know that look," he said.

"What?" she said, feigning innocence, turning away from him to look in the long oval mirror.

"You're up to something."

"I am not."

"Prudence."

She sighed. She knew she likely wouldn't be able to keep her plans from Hugo. Since they were children – Hugo being the second son of a marquess and marchioness who used to spend a great deal of time with her parents – the two of them had never been able to keep anything from one another. He knew all her secrets... and she his. It was a trust neither of them would ever break – especially due to the fact that if anyone were ever to discover Hugo's secret it would be the end of his life as he knew it.

"Very well. I have decided that I am tired of all that is threatening my family. No one seems to be able to do anything about it. My brother. The detective who did nothing but fall in love with and marry my sister. Any of his men, who are supposed to be the best in London. For goodness' sake, our top suspect ended up being our half-brother who married Lady Maria and proved his own innocence!"

"It is quite a convoluted conundrum," Hugo said, and Prudence couldn't help but smile at the way he twisted words from even a regular conversation into such poetry. "But what are you going to do about it?"

"I am going to solve this puzzle myself," she said, straightening and placing her bonnet on her head exactly as she liked it.

Hugo crossed his arms over his chest as he leaned against the wall in his meticulously organized room. "I do not like the sound of that."

"You know I am capable."

"You are not invincible."

"No," she agreed. "But sometimes the best man for the job is a woman."

He snorted at that, pushing off the wall and following her as she made her way toward the door.

"I know better than to try to stop you, but I do have one request."

"Which is?"

"That you tell me your plan and that you allow me to help you."

"Very well. I must start with investigating Lord Trundelle, though I am unsure how as of yet. Once I decide what the plan is, I will be sure to tell you."

"Promise?"

"Promise."

"Good. I know you have your own reasons for distrusting Lord Trundelle, but there is much talk about him, Prudence. From what I have heard, what people say about him, coupled with all that you suspect about him... you must be very careful."

"Always."

"Would it help if I tried to arrange a rematch for you with him?"

Prudence paused. She hadn't shared with Hugo her concern – that she had burned all her bridges with Henry Angelo and he would never arrange another match for her again, which was quite possibly her greatest fear. But she couldn't have finished the bout today or she would have lost everything.

"If both Angelo and Lord Trundelle are willing to arrange a rematch I would certainly be in favor," she said before her lips curled up in a smile. "In truth, Hugo, it was the most even match I have participated in for a very long time. While it was against Lord Trundelle, I cannot recall a time recently where I have forgotten everything else that has threatened my father or my brother or anyone in my family. And," she said, grinning triumphantly, "it reminded me that I am strong enough to do anything I set my mind to."

"Oh, Prudence," he said, following her out the door to walk her back home to Warwick House, which sat in the middle of London, surrounded by fences on all sides like a fortress. "What am I going to do with you?"

BENEDICT WEARILY LET himself in the door of his townhouse. Set on the edge of a row of townhouses, it had been in his family since he was a child. He had considered offering it to his brother, Martin, but something within him couldn't completely let go of it, and he had no desire to find another place to live. Not when he was comfortable here, where he held onto the memories of his parents.

There was enough change in his world without him having to add to it.

"Good afternoon, my lord," his butler greeted him, holding out a hand to take his jacket. Jefferson was well aware of Benedict's moods and said no more than what was required of him. Benedict nodded to him as he slid out of the garment and passed it to him, shaking his head as he made his way through the house back to his study, not bothering to go upstairs to change. It was not like he was going to be seeing anyone.

He was called to his desk and ledgers like some men were to the clubs and their drink. He couldn't help it. All his life, all he had ever wanted was to exact revenge in the best way he knew how – hurting men in their pocketbooks and reputations.

"Lord Trundelle, a gentleman came to call upon you while you were out. Lord Dennison," Jefferson said, and Benedict snorted, his lips curling up ever so slightly. So the new Lord Dennison was at least a touch more intelligent than the former one had been if he had realized this quickly just how much of his fortune he actually owed to Benedict and not, as the previous one had supposed, to the Duke of Warwick.

"What did you tell him?" Benedict asked, hearing the growl in his voice but knowing that Jefferson wouldn't take it personally.

"That you were out. He said he would try again tomorrow. I suggested he make an appointment, but he refused."

"When he returns tomorrow, tell him I am out once more, no matter where I am," Benedict said, to which Jefferson nodded without question. Benedict would keep Dennison sweating until he figured out the man's nature.

He tried to review his ledgers, as he did at the beginning of every work session when he sat at his desk before them, but he found that for once he couldn't concentrate. All he could think about was his fencing match. Damn, but he wished the lad hadn't been scared away, as he must have been. For what other reason would he leave so abruptly, and with such panic in his eyes? Eyes that called out to Benedict in a way that scared him, for it stirred something deep in his soul, something he had long considered dormant. Emotion.

He had tried to ask Angelo more about this Robertson once he had run away, but Angelo had shrugged and told him he hadn't much to share.

"He first came to me about a year ago," Angelo had said. "He was quite well-trained, by his father apparently, although he wouldn't tell me just *who* his father is, which is interesting for there is not many a highly skilled fencer I do not know. He asked me for training, which I provided, as well as the opportunity to bout. He seemed so young, so untested, that I initially said no, sure he would be bested every time, but he proved me wrong – as well as everyone else."

"Interesting," Benedict had murmured. While he kept a great deal of secrets himself, he didn't like the thought of others keeping such secrets from him. "If you find out anything else, do tell me."

"Would you like me to set up another match, my lord?" Angelo had asked him, one brow raised.

"Yes. With the lad again," Benedict had said, causing Angelo to stare at him in curiosity.

"After he forfeited as he did?"

"Yes," Benedict had said, setting his jaw. "He beat me."

"He gave up the match."

"He was beating me. And nobody beats me. Set up the match."

Angelo had nodded, and then Benedict had left before any of the other dandies arrived. Not only did he hate the crowds, but he couldn't stand how they all attended Angelo's simply because it was the popular thing to do and not because they loved the sport. Not like he did. Fencing ran through his veins, and he couldn't get enough of it.

What was it about Robertson that was bothering him?

He pushed it all from his mind as he returned to sit behind his desk and dipped his quill pen in the inkwell, flipping through the pages of his ledgers before he found what Lord Dennison owed.

And smiled.

It brought him nearly as much joy as the pages which included the words 'the Duke of Warwick.' Not that he had anything against the new Duke of Warwick, besides the fact that he shared the same blood as the man who had completely ruined Benedict's life.

Benedict had achieved his goal of returning his father's fortunes to his coffers. There was but one last stage of his plan, one which would bring down the entire Warwick family.

Too bad the previous duke wouldn't be here to see it.

CHAPTER 3

"*E*mma. Juliana."

Prudence forced her brightest smile onto her face as she greeted her sister-in-law as well as her sister. Juliana may no longer live with them, not now that she was married to the detective and lived in Holborn of all places, but she was here nearly as often as Emma used to be before she had married Prudence and Juliana's brother.

Emma and Juliana had always been the closest of friends, although it hadn't surprised Prudence in the least when Emma and their eldest brother, Giles, had fallen in love. It had been clear all along that they would be perfect for one another. The only other person who had guessed was her grandmother. The two of them had discussed it well before Emma had been trapped out on the balcony with Giles. Another moment that the two of them thought was kept secret from anyone else.

"Good afternoon," Emma said, beaming from the rocking chair in the corner of the parlor, as she held little Grace in her arms. She had given birth just two weeks prior and looked completely exhausted but also quite happy – a paradox that Prudence couldn't quite wrap her head around. "Where were you today?"

"Fencing with Hugo," she said, always cognizant to keep her lies as truthful as possible.

"Were you, again?" Juliana said, her green eyes, so like Prudence's own, flashing. "You have spent a great deal of time with him lately, Pru. Is there something we should know about?"

"Absolutely not. My maid was with us the entire time, and you know as well as anyone, Jules, that Hugo and I are only friends and always will be."

Juliana bit her lip. "I know you have never felt that way about him, but 'tis a pity, seeing as you are so well matched in almost every other way. Marriages have been based on much less."

"Says the woman who married a man far below her station in life, risking everything for love."

Juliana dipped her head with a small smile. "You are right, of course."

"I always am," Prudence said, holding her head high. "Where is Mother?"

"Already preparing for tonight."

"Tonight?"

"There is a dinner party at Lord Nenson's. She said that you were joining her," Juliana said, tilting her head, and Prudence nearly stamped her foot on the ground, so annoyed she was with her own inability to remember an engagement.

"I do not blame you for not being interested," Juliana continued. "Lord and Lady Nenson are insufferable bores. The last time Mother forced me along with her I had to fake a megrim to leave."

"Juliana!" Emma exclaimed, looking at her wide-eyed for a moment as though about to chastise her before the two of them burst into laughter. Prudence just rolled her eyes and began to walk toward the stairs, knowing it was too late now to back out, as much as she wanted to.

Except... Lord Nenson's townhouse was also on Portman Square. She knew – from her own investigating – that Lord Trundelle's townhouse was on Portman Square. This just might be the perfect opportunity to put her plan into action.

She would have no time to inform Hugo of the change in plans as promised – not unless he would be at the dinner himself, which she was sure wouldn't be the case, for he would never attend with such company even if they had invited him. She couldn't get into that much trouble when she was already so close to his house – could she?

* * *

A FEW HOURS LATER, Prudence wasn't sure that her chance was ever going to come.

She had hoped that perhaps tonight they would eat earlier than a usual *ton* dinner event, but of course, that wasn't the case. No, Lady Nenson had to draw out this dinner so long that Prudence nearly fainted in hunger, let alone nearly miss the chance to put her plan into action.

She could have left early in the dinner but had thought her best bet was to wait until it was not only late enough that she would have the cover of greater darkness, but also that most of the guests – including her mother – would have imbibed enough that they might not notice she took longer to attend to her needs in the ladies' room than she normally did.

As it was, she was certain she wasn't going to have a particularly great amount of time, for her mother was sure to want to leave shortly. Prudence hoped that the other guests had a decent amount of gossip to share this evening to keep her mother entertained.

"I shall be but a moment, Mother," she said in her mother's ear before slipping out the door, noting with pleasure that her mother barely noticed her exit, so intent she was on the story one of the other women was telling. Prudence had worn navy this evening, which her mother had commented on, of course, telling her that it was *not* her most becoming color, but then she was used to Prudence not always dressing as she would prefer. Prudence, of course, did not overly care what her mother thought and dressed as she pleased instead.

She had tried to determine all the best exits earlier in the evening, and she was able to slip out of a servant's entrance at the back, taking to the mews between the houses. From what she was aware, Lord Trundelle's house was the at the end of the row, which was three down, she counted as she went, before standing back to review the house and determine the best way to enter.

She walked to a window, dragging a small bench over so that she could peer in, wincing at the scraping noise it made. She was pleased to find the room dark within, not even a fire lit in the grate. Good. No one would be about. She tugged on the window to see if it would open. At first it seemed stuck, but fortunately, it didn't appear to be locked, and with a few grunts and a fair bit of strength, she was able to push it open. Once it got past the block, however, the force she had pressed against it was too great and the window flew up and hit the top of the frame with a bang that made her cringe.

She ducked down and waited to see if anyone had noticed the sound, relieved when she didn't hear anyone approach.

She placed her hand on the sill and hoisted herself up and through, ending up on a soft rug with what she hoped was a soundless landing. It was cold in the room, without a fire in the grate and the door shut, and she padded over to place her ear against the door to determine if there was anyone outside it. With any luck, Lord Trundelle would be out at a club or with friends. Not that he seemed like a man who *had* many friends, but he had been rather close with Lord Dennison, had he not been, before Dennison was killed during his attempt to retrieve Lady Maria?

Of course, a friendship with Lord Dennison said very little about a man's reputation.

Prudence gently eased the door open, pleased to find the corridor empty. From what she knew, Lord Trundelle lived alone, and likely wouldn't require a great deal of servants to look after his needs. Hopefully, most of them would be abed already, the hour having already passed midnight.

She tiptoed down the corridor as softly as she could, though her footsteps were hurried until she reached various doorways. Most were open, and it took but two attempts until she found what she was looking for – his study. There was a fire burning in this grate, so she knew she would have to be quick.

Prudence turned her head when she heard voices, but it seemed the conversation was being held at the front of the house. Lord Trundelle was within, then, speaking to a servant, or perhaps even guests. She would have preferred that he be out of the house, but at least they should keep him occupied for a time.

The light from the fire cast a glow enough for her to see, although a candle to search with would have helped. She certainly couldn't take the time to light anything, and if anyone happened upon her, it would most obviously give her away.

She took a seat in the large mahogany and leather chair behind the matching desk, both as masculine and imposing as the man himself. He liked to feel strong, then, did he, she thought as she ran her hands over the bronze mounts on the sides of the chair? She wondered how strong he had felt when he had gone after her father – if he had been the culprit.

She began to flip through the book in front of her, which appeared well used. There were names and numbers marked throughout in a strong, thick, meticulous hand, which could only be Lord Trundelle's. Were they debits or credits? She wondered. No, she finally realized. They were debts. Debts that appeared to be owed to Lord Trundelle.

On the top of the open page was written Lord Dennison's name, which she found odd, for were they not friends who had been working against her father and then her brother? There was also a note as to who the debts had been transferred from – the Duke of Warwick. That was odd. Though *which* Duke of Warwick, it didn't say. She looked to the door before she slowly began to tear out the page and slipped it into her bodice. Lord Trundelle would obviously realize the theft as soon as he returned to his ledger, but he would have no idea she had even been in his study.

The next page held nothing of interest, and she flipped to another page again, before her brother's name stared at her from the top this time – Giles Remington, the Duke of Warwick. But what did that mean? She placed her finger on the page to read more, but before she could continue, a voice came from the doorframe.

"Find anything interesting?"

Prudence nearly jumped out of the chair as her head snapped up, taking in the tall, broad frame that filled nearly the entire doorway.

A frame more formidable, more masculine than any other she knew. And the face on top of it was staring at her with such grim annoyance that she shuddered despite herself.

She had been caught.

By Lord Trundelle.

* * *

BENEDICT STOOD STARING at the woman who currently occupied his seat.

He crossed his arms over his chest as she observed him like an animal who had been caught and knew she was trapped, with no way out.

He had to hand it to her, however. While he saw her shudder, she didn't show any sign of backing down, no fear in her eyes.

Instead, she squared her shoulders and stood up to look at him as though she was welcoming him into her drawing room.

"Lord Trundelle," she said calmly, and he willed her to walk forward into the light so he could ascertain her identity. Her voice was low, deep, throaty, and it shook him right to his core.

It also sounded awfully familiar.

"I do not suppose you would like to tell me just what you are doing in my study at such an hour when you were not actually invited into my house?"

"I could come up with a lie and hope that you would believe it, however we would both know that I was merely hiding the truth."

"So instead you will say nothing?"

"I think that is best."

He narrowed his eyes at her.

"I would suggest you leave and hope that I never lay eyes on you again."

"Very well," she said, rounding the desk and walking toward him. He wondered what she was doing until she came to a stop in front of him and said, "If you will excuse me," and he realized he was blocking the doorway.

She was close enough that her scent washed over him,

one that reminded him of warm chocolate in the morning. It filled him with a sense of uneasy comfort and peace that he did not entirely welcome.

He was just about to step out of her way when she opened her mouth again.

"Before I go, I have a question."

He lifted a brow in response.

"Why were you working with Lord Dennison when he actually owed you money?"

"That is not any of your concern."

"It is, in a way."

"How so?"

"Because…" she trailed off and her eyes, which had been staring into his, the intensity of their green rather disconcerting, flicked to the side as though she was only now hiding something from him. "It affects my family."

He took a good look at her then. Her countenance, the way she held herself had seemed oddly familiar to him even when she had stood from the chair, but he hadn't been able to place her looks. Her eyes shouldn't be hard to forget, and yet while he felt that he had seen them before, and that it had been at some time recently, he couldn't place them.

But there was something else.

It was the slant of her cheekbones, her nose that was slightly too prominent for her face. She…

"You are Remington's sister."

She stepped back slightly.

"I am, yes."

"What's your name?"

"I would prefer not to answer."

She had backbone, this one.

"As you have allowed yourself entrance into my house, I believe I deserve to at least know your identity."

She took a step back into the room away from him, but

he followed, keeping his eyes upon her. Her mouth remained shut.

"You are not going anywhere until you tell me just who you are. And if you do not tell me, I will simply discover the truth another way."

She swallowed as though realizing just how serious he was.

"Very well. Lady Prudence Remington."

"Well, Lady Prudence," he said, taking another step toward her, although this time she didn't back away from him, meaning that they were almost nose to nose – which was, in fact, the closest he had actually come to another person in more time than he would care to admit. "I do not suppose you would care to show me what you shoved down your gown before you knew I was here?"

Her eyes flashed and her cheeks flamed, but she admitted nothing.

"I did no such thing."

"You are a thief."

"You are a liar."

"As are you."

"At least I am not a murderer," she bit out, before her lips clamped together as though she realized she had gone too far.

Benedict stepped back, but just for a moment.

"That is quite an accusation, and one that I do not completely understand."

"I speak only the truth of what I know – that there is a very good chance you murdered my father."

He allowed his lips to stretch into a thin smile. "While I cannot say that I am overly vexed at your father's death, Lady Prudence, I unfortunately cannot take the credit for it."

"Well, we have already ascertained that you are a liar, so unfortunately your words mean nothing."

"Hand over what you stole, Lady Prudence."

"I will not."

"Well, we've made progress if you are no longer denying that you have taken something from me."

He saw the heat in her gaze, then, knew he was causing her great ire, but he no longer cared.

He stepped toward her, and before she even knew what was happening, he used one hand to pull the fabric of her bodice away from her bosom and pushed the other to search within.

As she lifted her arm to bat him away furiously, there was a gasp from behind him, and he knew with a sinking feeling, even before turning around, just who was there.

And it could only mean sure disaster.

CHAPTER 4

*P*rudence had thought her earlier experience at Angelo's was one of the most mortifying of her life.

But nothing could top this one. She was in Lord Trundelle's study, his hand down her bodice, no explanation immediately apparent, while three women and a man looked on.

Oh, goodness.

"Benedict!" the first woman cried, and as she surged forward, Prudence unfortunately recognized her.

"Aunt Emily," he said with a voice that was surprisingly calm considering their predicament. "This is not what it looks like."

"So you do not have your hand down this young woman's bodice, in your study, alone and unchaperoned, at one o'clock in the morning?"

"Is it truly that late?" Prudence said, attempting to keep her voice light even as her heart hammered in her chest — a chest that only now did Lord Trundle swiftly remove his hand from. "I really must be going."

"Lady Prudence!"

Oh, bollocks.

The second woman stepped around the first, and Prudence realized with a sinking heart it was Lady Lightingale, who had been at the Nenson's dinner party and considered herself a friend of her mother's.

"Lady Lightingale, wonderful to see you again."

"Your mother is looking for you, Lady Prudence. We thought you were lost in the house, not... not..."

She couldn't seem to find the words as her mouth gaped open and closed, while her eyes widened over and again.

Prudence tried to smile, but she was certain it emerged as something more of a grimace.

"I can assure you that this was not planned," she said.

As Lord Trundelle's brother, Mr. Martin Gallagher, stepped to the side, his wife, Mrs. Amelia Gallagher, followed along with him. They wore matching expressions of worry, although for whom, Prudence wasn't entirely certain. She was acquainted with them from *ton* events, although she couldn't say she had ever had an overly long conversation with either of them. "I thought I was entering the home of a friend, you see, but then Lord Trundelle caught me and believed I was stealing from him. I was not, of course."

"Benedict?" said Mr. Gallagher with some hesitation. From what Prudence knew, he was a jovial man, liked by all – the complete opposite of his brother. "Why would you think that Lady Prudence would have any other reason for being here?"

"Unfortunately," Lord Trundelle said through gritted teeth, "that is something that only Lady Prudence can answer."

"Excuse me for one moment," Lady Lightingale said, lifting a finger, before backing out of the room, and Prudence knew there was but one place she would likely be going and one person she would be fetching, who she would feel she must bring into this scene – and it was not going to be a good situation for Prudence.

"None of you are even supposed to be here," Lord Trundelle said, his cheeks, which had been a rather pale shade, reddening.

"That is hardly a thing to say to your aunt. We were travelling right past your house on the way home from the theatre. How could we not stop to see you?"

"It was midnight. I would have not minded one bit had you continued on your way."

His aunt shook her head at him. "Where did I go wrong in raising you?" she asked, and from the look on Lord Trundelle's face, Prudence guessed he had much to say in response but realized that now was not the time to tell her what he thought.

"I told you already, this is not what it looks like. Lady Prudence here—" he turned to her then, an arm stretched out toward her, and Prudence realized with satisfaction that he could not continue. For to tell his family why she was at his house would be informing them that she had reason to believe he was responsible for her father's death, and he certainly would not want to share her suspicions with anyone else.

"Became lost," she supplied helpfully, and he sighed as he ran a hand through his hair.

"Yes. She became lost."

"Prudence!"

Prudence cringed at her mother's voice. Her mother was not a woman overly given to a frenzy – at least, not when she was in the company of anyone who she felt mattered – but apparently these were extenuating circumstances.

"Whatever could you possibly be doing here?" she asked, her gaze whipping between Prudence and Lord Trundelle.

"It is a long story," Prudence said tersely, hoping that her mother would gather from her intense stare that the story was one she would prefer to tell her on their way home and not in front of Lord Trundelle and his family.

She noticed that Lady Lightingale, obviously quite interested in being privy to the conclusion of this affair, had returned along with her mother. She cringed, for Lady Lightingale was not one known for her discretion.

"Not to worry," Lady Emily said, holding her head high, "my nephew will be sure to right all this."

"Aunt Emily," Benedict said, no longer disguising his true emotions as he bit out the words. "The conclusion of this business is none of your concern."

"Of course it is!" she exclaimed. "Benedict, you know there is only one option now. What else are we to do?"

He sighed again, and Prudence could practically feel his distress radiating out and toward her. Panic, a sensation she was not entirely used to, started to beat in her own breast. Deep within, she had known what this would mean the moment they were discovered, but she hadn't allowed the thought into her consciousness until Lady Emily had spoken it aloud.

For Prudence certainly had no wish to be tied to Lord Trundelle, no matter what position they had found themselves in. For once, she was quick to take up his defense.

"I am sure we can come to a solution that we can all be happy with," she said quickly, and Lord Trundelle stared at her with hooded eyes.

"I will speak to your brother tomorrow and we will come to a resolution."

Prudence opened her mouth to deny his suggestion, but then realized that if he did as he said, it would likely result in the most positive outcome. Giles would never allow her to marry such a man. She was sure of it.

"Very well," she said instead, as she began to edge around Lord Trundelle to leave the room, tilting her head in a signal for her mother to follow behind her. "I shall tell Giles to look forward to your visit."

She slipped around his imposing figure, a shudder running through her once more at his close proximity, before fleeing the room, her mother following behind her. She wished her grandmother was there, for she would know what to say to extract them from this situation.

It was then she realized that she had no idea how to find the front door.

"To your right," she heard a deep voice in her ear, and turned her head to see that he was standing there again, ready to take her arm to walk her to the door while her mother had been drawn back by Lady Lightingale, who was speaking rapidly in her ear as her gaze wandered between Prudence and Lord Trundelle.

She paused. She had no wish to show him any kind of sympathy, and yet… something about him drew her to him. Perhaps it was the haunted look in his eyes, the wounded soul he possessed, but it was a desire she would never share with anyone, for it was dark, one that made no sense whatsoever. He was not a man she should ever want to dally with, especially when she knew what he was capable of, the crimes that she was trying to prove he committed. When his hand had been down her bodice, however, if she hadn't been so scared that he would find what she had hidden there, she might have actually… *welcomed* his touch. What could that possibly say about her?

Her thoughts were disrupted when she felt the crinkle in the bodice of her gown, and, knowing that he heard it at the same time, she winced.

"Good night, then, Lady Prudence," he said when they reached the front door, the sarcasm in his voice as obvious as any she had ever heard before. "How lovely of you to drop in."

"Goodnight," she said to the group as a whole. "I am ever so sorry for the inconvenience."

She felt her mother's stare on her as they walked down the stairs, in front of the eyes of all at Lord and Lady Nenson's party to see.

It was then that Prudence realized just how truly dire this situation was.

* * *

BENEDICT DIDN'T ENJOY CALLING upon other members of the *ton*.

But he had never dreaded a visit quite as much as he did this one.

It seemed that all in the Remington household were aware of the reason for his visit, as even the butler appeared to eye him with derision before he led him through the massive house and eventually to the duke's study.

So far, there was no sign of Lady Prudence, nor any of the rest of the family.

Until he walked through the door of the study and there she was, sitting in one of the obviously new cream chairs in front of the duke's desk, her brother occupying the chair behind the desk and across from her.

Benedict had been in here but once before, as the previous duke preferred to conduct his business, if one could call it that, elsewhere and away from his family. In fact, the previous duke had spent most of his life away from his family.

Clearly, Remington had made some changes. This room had been imprinted in Benedict's mind but now, gone were the heavy curtains that had made Benedict feel as though the room was closing in on him, and there was no sign of the previous duke's portrait, which had hung above the fireplace like a mirror projecting the duke himself back at him.

It was much more welcoming now, even if Benedict knew that the duke would not intend for him to feel at ease.

"I would say it is good to see you, Trundelle, but I cannot recall the last time our paths crossed."

"That would be because you ran away until your father died."

The duke, who had been sitting behind his desk with his arms crossed, visibly bristled, and Benedict had to prevent himself from smiling. One point for him, then.

"My family's affairs are none of your concern."

"I am glad to hear it."

"Oh?"

"For that means there is no true reason for my presence here."

The duke's eyes narrowed, and Benedict knew he was likely not helping himself, but he could not allow snide comments to go unremarked upon. Lady Prudence had, to this point, remained silent, although he noticed her brows lift when he challenged the duke.

"You and my sister were caught in a compromising position last night."

"I told all who found us, and I will tell you again, that it was not how it appeared."

"So Prudence has informed me," the duke said, his hands curling around the ends of his desk chair. "It leaves me with a great deal of uncertainty on our next steps. You both know that the correct thing to do would be for you and Prudence to marry."

Lady Prudence didn't hide her choke while Benedict felt the unease rise within him. For he had no wish to marry – Lady Prudence or any other woman.

"It really isn't necessary, Giles—" she began.

Benedict remained silent. He was in quite the spot. For as much as he could protest the marriage, if this is what the Remington family called for, how was he supposed to deny them?

"Prudence," her brother cut her off, "even you must realize the scandal this will cause."

"More of a scandal than Juliana marrying a detective?" she asked, with a raised brow. "More of a scandal than when the woman you were supposed to marry until you cried off for your sister's best friend ended up married to our half-brother instead?"

Well, that was news to Benedict, although he wasn't one to keep up with *ton* gossip.

Giles turned a shade of red that could be attributed to anger or embarrassment – Benedict wasn't entirely sure which.

"How the mighty can fall," Benedict murmured, which caused Giles to turn a withering glare upon him.

"We were not overly high to begin with," he said. "You met my father."

"I most certainly did," Benedict said tersely, not caring to remember accompanying his father to Warwick House, only to see the man he so looked up to leave so defeated.

"I do not care about scandal if it means preventing a marriage that would be sure misery – for both of you," Giles said, looking from one of them to the other. "Will it cause great scandal if you do not marry? Yes, of course it will. And to answer your question, Pru, it would be another stain upon the family, yes, but the rest of us can withstand it. More important would be the fact that you would surely be ruined. I cannot imagine another man offering for you – at least anytime soon – knowing the position you were found in with Trundelle. Especially without any explanation.

There was no reason for you to have been in his bloody house."

"No reason that can be explained, anyway," Benedict supplied, and Giles turned a rather murderous gaze upon him.

"The three of us in this room know what brought Prudence there. And no matter what society says, I will certainly not marry her to a murderer."

"Ah, the family blood runs true," Benedict muttered.

"Do you admit it, then?" Giles asked. "Did you murder our father?"

Benedict tipped back his chair as though the accusation meant nothing to him, even though in truth it said quite a bit that more than one person had no trouble believing him to be a murderer. He was well aware that he was certainly not a favored son among the nobility, but that they would all so easily believe him a killer – even if the victim had been the Duke of Warwick – was something else entirely.

He allowed the front legs of the chair to drop back down to the floor.

"Of course I didn't kill him," he said rather viciously. "You, of anyone, should know what it means to be accused of murder."

When the duke had reappeared in society following his father's death, he had been the most likely suspect for what most considered to be murder. It wasn't until the remainder of the family began to be threatened as well and an attempt had been made upon Giles' life that all had realized another was likely the culprit.

Benedict could see the unease on the faces of the siblings, and finally he threw his hands up in the air. "If you need proof, I was in the country the night he was murdered."

"That is not what the detective said," Giles said, his brows creasing, and Benedict rolled his eyes.

"Yes, the detective that has been doing such a fine job for you, hasn't he now?"

"You are speaking of my brother-in-law," the duke said mildly.

"A position you are also offering me," Benedict countered, and the duke frowned, exchanging a glance with Prudence.

"Nothing – and I mean absolutely nothing – matters more to me than keeping my family safe," the duke said, fixing his blue-eyed stare on Benedict. "I will risk scandal and the chance that my sister might forever be living under my roof if it will keep her from any harm."

"I am glad that option is met with such acceptance, Giles," Lady Prudence said wryly from the chair beside Benedict, but her brother ignored her.

"Out of all within our family, this scandal, of course, will have the greatest impact on Prudence's life," the duke continued. "If, and only if, you can prove to us that you are innocent in my father's murder, then it will be up to Prudence. She can choose to welcome scandal and reject you, or she can choose to take her chances with you."

Benedict could see Lady Prudence staring open-mouthed at her brother, but he couldn't back away from Giles' challenge.

"I do not recall offering for her."

"I do not recall giving you a choice."

Benedict sat back, looking from Lady Prudence to her brother and back again now.

"I will offer you one bit of advice," the duke said, leaning back and running his eyes over Benedict as though determining his worth. "If you are concerned about having to share your life with someone, that is not a worry with Prudence. Never before have I met a woman who has filled her time with so many tasks herself that she has little time for any other."

Prudence did not seem insulted by her brother this time as she shrugged. "It is true. I never before thought I would have much time for a husband."

Benedict wished he had longer to consider this. He didn't like being rushed into decisions, but he also knew that at this point he hadn't much choice remaining before him.

He considered that if it was as Lady Prudence and the duke said, and he and the woman could continue to live their own, separate lives despite being married, then perhaps this could be the perfect opportunity to fulfill his duty without having to actually try to appease a woman.

"Very well," he finally said, hardly believing the words were coming from his mouth. "We may marry."

She stared at him, her green eyes giving no indication of what she was thinking.

"Do not sound too excited, my lord," she said, her eyes dancing, but it appeared that her brother'd had enough.

"Just tell us, Prudence," he said. "What do you decide?"

CHAPTER 5

*P*rudence tried not to fidget in her seat. She had been so sure that Giles would simply tell Lord Trundelle to turn around and leave. She had never considered the possibility that he might actually entertain the idea of a marriage to her. She wasn't sure what it said about either of them that the sole reason he had been persuaded was the thought that he wouldn't have to spend much time with her.

At least Giles had given her the opportunity to make the decision. She closed her eyes briefly, unable to take Lord Trundelle's stare any longer as he waited for her response.

She had no desire to marry him, of course. But she was also feeling a great deal of guilt at the thought that if she didn't, she would be bringing further shame upon her family. They had already been through so much, were still facing a threat that had them all constantly under tension. Poor Emma had spent most of the time she was expecting within the confines of Warwick House, for Giles was far too concerned about what might have happened if she left.

That made her think of baby Grace, and Prudence knew

then what she had to do – and maybe she could help her family in the process.

"Very well," she said, squaring her shoulders and looking Lord Trundelle in the eye. If she didn't know any better, that was a smirk on his face, a smirk that was telling her he assumed she would back away from him, be too cowardly to agree to a marriage to him.

How little he knew of her.

"I will marry you."

She watched in satisfaction as Lord Trundelle gripped the arms of his chair, his smirk slowly fading from his face until he was staring at her in near horror.

"You will marry me," he repeated.

"That is what I said."

"If he can prove his innocence," Giles interjected.

"Of course I am innocent," Lord Trundelle bit out, his gaze darkening, and Prudence wondered if that thumping in her chest was her heart skipping a beat in fear.

Surely, if he was innocent, he couldn't be that bad – could he?

* * *

BENEDICT COULD HARDLY BELIEVE that it was just yesterday he had participated in one of the closest, most exhilarating fencing matches of his life, and had been so focused on meeting his opponent in a rematch.

Little had he known that in less than a day he would be saddled with a wife and a scandal – although not in that order.

He knocked on the door of a house he knew well but seldom visited, one that he paid a great deal for, despite his brother's insistence that he would be just fine living elsewhere.

It was not Martin's fault that he had been born two years later than Benedict. He was, however, doing the job that Benedict had refused – to marry and produce sons who would carry on the line after they were both gone.

Benedict supposed some of that was changing now, although he was still very clear that he would never take any action that would lead to children of his own.

He may be agreeing to marry, but he had quickly decided that he wouldn't break the promise he had made to himself.

There was no need to consummate a marriage unless a man was trying to beget heirs. And that was already taken care of – by Martin.

"How are my favorite nephews?" he asked as two of Martin's children, Oliver and Alexander, raced by.

"Fine, Uncle Benedict!" they said, two of the only people who he allowed to actually see his true self – them and their sister, Liliana.

"Benedict," said his brother cheerfully as he emerged from one of the back rooms, as though he hadn't been present for the dramatics the previous night. "This is a nice surprise. I have now seen you twice in two days. That might be more than in the entirety of last month."

"It has been a day already, as you might imagine," Benedict said, stepping past his brother and into the room. "Today did not go as planned."

"Let me guess," Martin said, tapping one finger on his nose. "You are now promised to the Lady Prudence."

Benedict rubbed his forehead. "Yes."

"I figured as much," he said. "There are not many other options following the position we discovered you in last night."

"That was rather unfortunate," Benedict said, "although we were telling the truth."

For the most part at least.

"Still," Martin said, shaking his head, "when a woman such as Lady Lightingale sees you in such a circumstance, you have little chance in how to extract yourself."

"So I have learned," Benedict said dryly.

"Would you care to tell us what actually happened?" Martin asked, and Benedict looked around at the three shrieking children circling the room.

"I do not believe now is the time for this particular vein of storytelling. But needless to say, I have to prove that I did not kill the former Duke of Warwick, and then all will be forgiven, and we can move on."

"Kill the duke?" Martin's eyes nearly bugged out of his head. "Why would you ever kill the duke?"

"I did hate him," Benedict said, pausing for a moment, remembering Martin didn't know the full story of their family's past. "Though not enough to kill him. I am not a killer. As it happens, the Remingtons do not currently trust anyone outside the family, given their current situation. They feel that anyone could be a risk, and therefore they would like to know my whereabouts the night the duke was killed."

"You can provide that?" Martin asked, aghast, and, as he usually did, Benedict had both pity for his brother as well as a gladness that Martin didn't know the truth of the world as Benedict did. He had been able to maintain some innocence for his brother throughout his childhood and well into adulthood.

"I can. I remember the duke's death, for it had a great significance on my... business dealings. I was in the country at the time, and I believe I had met with my steward as well as another in the area. I should be able to provide confirmation."

Martin was shaking his head in wonder. "I never thought

I would see this day. You. Married. Proving yourself for a woman."

"Nor did I, Martin," Benedict said, suddenly wanting nothing more than to return home and not have to talk to anyone else for the rest of the day. "Nor did I."

* * *

"You cannot be serious," Juliana said, apparently voicing the concerns of the entirety of Prudence's family, for everyone else was nodding along with her, with the exception of their mother, who sat there stoically.

Prudence looked around at all who had gathered in the drawing room.

Giles, his wife Emma, Prudence's mother, and her grandmother all lived in the house, of course, and then Juliana and her detective husband, Matthew Archibald had arrived. Even her half-brother, the bastard son of her father's, was in attendance with his new wife, Lady Maria.

Lady Lightingale had been persuaded to keep her silence – for a week, until appropriate announcements could be made.

It had been five days since Prudence had been caught with Lord Trundelle, four since he had promised to provide evidence proving his innocence in her father's death.

It had been but half a day since Benedict had arrived on their doorstep again, providing that very proof to Giles. He had secured the word of his steward that they had conversed at Lord Trundelle's country residence the afternoon of her father's death. He also had the word of another man who had confirmed he had seen Lord Trundelle riding across his grounds.

How was she to refute that?

"Not to worry," she said, lifting her chin as she stared at them all. "I can take care of myself."

Her grandmother tapped her cane on the ground, her wise stare raking over Prudence, leaving her more exposed than if she had been sitting there undressed. Her grandmother understood her in a way no one else ever did, and sometimes it scared Prudence how alike she was to the woman.

"Why would you agree to this, girl? You have no need for a husband."

"No," Prudence said slowly, "but this family also has no need for another scandal."

"Who cares about that?" Juliana asked, as her little dog, Lucy, ran around her feet. Thankfully, she had left the rest of her menagerie at home. "We have weathered enough scandals already."

"Yes, but this one? This is different," Prudence said, shaking her head. "Mother might never be invited to another event again. Emma, you could be further ostracized from society than you already are."

Prudence knew that one was true and also knew that it would bother Emma. "And think of Grace. I do not want her to go through life believing there to be something wrong with her or her family when I could have fixed everything by making a different choice."

"Surely you do not think that anyone would hold a family's actions against a little child," Emma said, but even Giles looked at her with some unease.

"Emma, you know what society is like," he said, and she sighed in acceptance.

"Prudence, what about Lord Trundelle himself?" Juliana pressed. "He hardly ever shows himself in society and no one has anything particularly fond to say about him. How would being married to him be better than your current situation?"

"Just because he does not go into society does not mean that I cannot," Prudence said, wondering whether she was trying to convince her family or herself. "I do truly believe that he wants the two of us to lead separate lives. Which works just fine for me. I can continue to live life as I choose, and I will not be a burden to your family, Giles."

"I hope you would never think that of yourself. When I said that you might never marry, I didn't mean—"

"I know," she said softly. "I know you wouldn't mind providing for me. But I would prefer you didn't have to."

"As long as you do not have any thought that he might be cruel," Lady Maria said softly, and Prudence winced, for with all that was happening, she had forgotten to be sensitive to Lady Maria and the threat she had faced in her first marriage to Lord Dennison, with a husband whose only intention had been to cause her pain – and who had been tied to Lord Trundelle.

"If it helps, I have never heard any talk of Lord Trundelle's action with women – in any sense, cruel or otherwise. I know that he is ruthless in business, that he has no issue in taking advantage of other's despair, but as far as being anything like Lord Dennison, I have no knowledge."

Prudence nodded. "Thank you, Giles. That is good to know."

"I can look into it before your actual marriage," Matthew said. "I can also tell you that we haven't been able to find any evidence that he might have been responsible for the duke's death or Juliana's abduction, beyond what Lord Dennison said, and he was hardly a reputable source."

"I do have something for you that might help," Prudence said, passing Matthew the paper she had stolen from Lord Trundelle's ledger. "Giles, you will likely also be interested in reviewing it. It seems that Lord Trundelle purchased Lord

Dennison's vowels from Father. They were all in some kind of gambling circle together, it appears."

"Lord Trundelle is a gambler?" Emma asked, but Matthew was already shaking his head.

"No. We did look into that already. He waited for the other men to gamble, bought up their vowels, and came for them at a time when they would have no choice but to pay. It was quite a scheme but there is no law against what he was doing."

"I see," she said.

"He might not be honorable, but from I can tell, he has done nothing criminal," said Matthew, and Prudence nodded.

It appeared she no longer had any choice.

She would be marrying Lord Trundelle, whether she liked it or not.

CHAPTER 6

*B*enedict sat at the head of his long dining room table – a place he was rather unfamiliar with.

For he never had company.

And he hadn't been planning to start.

He was making one exception for tonight.

His wedding night.

A night that he had long ago decided was a dream that no longer existed. Instead, he had accepted the fact that he would forever eat alone, in his study, until the day he left this world.

He hoped that his wife would quickly realize the truth of the situation.

His wife.

She sat at the other end of the table, moving around the food on her plate as she not-so-surreptitiously eyed the room. Benedict supposed it *was* rather dated, as he had made no changes to it since his mother had redecorated before he was old enough to remember, but then, what was the point? He had made sure the heavy gold curtains were no longer full of dust, and there was nothing wrong with the dining room table or chairs – they were just a dark, heavy wood with black leather that *were* rather uncomfortable. He supposed he could tell Lady Prudence that if she preferred to replace some of the macabre scenes and ancient, disapproving ancestors staring down at them from around the room, she was more than welcome to.

"The ceremony was nice enough," said Lady Prudence – well, he supposed it was Lady Trundelle now.

Benedict raised an eyebrow. Was she truly going to try to make polite conversation?

"Especially considering that no one was invited and the two of us do not even know one another," she added.

Well, at least she wasn't going to pretend that nothing was amiss in this farce of a marriage. The ceremony had been short, to the point, with no one save their family as witnesses. He had been rather startled when he had seen Lady Prudence, although he had been sure not to react. She was an attractive woman, that he couldn't deny, but there had been something... more to her today. Her dress had been lighter, her chestnut hair softer, her green eyes glowing, although more with challenge than anything else.

She still had the same stiff backbone that she always did, and he couldn't help but admire that about her, though he made sure not to look up and provide her any opportunity to recognize his emotion.

"I didn't think you'd do it," he grumbled, stabbing a piece of beef and stuffing it into his mouth before he said anything else.

"Do what?" she asked, looking up in surprise. "Marry you?"

He nodded, unable to say any more with the size of the bite he had taken.

"I said I would," she said, her brow furrowing. "So, therefore, I did. I am a woman of my word, Lord Trundelle. That, you should soon realize."

"Sounds odd from you."

"What is that?"

"Lord Trundelle."

"It is your name, is it not? What would you prefer that I call you? What is your first name again? I must have heard it but cannot recall."

"Benedict."

"Very well. Benedict it is. Unless you have another name that you favor?"

He shook his head. His brother had always called him by his given name, and there was no one else in his life close enough to use any other.

"You may call me Prudence. Those close to me call me Pru, but that is your choice."

He studied her then, realized that she was rambling, which could only mean that she must be nervous.

"Why are you scared?" he asked, taking a sip of his drink.

"I am not scared."

"You sound as though you are."

"There is very little that scares me, Lord— Benedict."

"Is it the wedding night?" he asked.

She said nothing, although her eyes widened slightly, and he knew he had found his answer. "Not to worry. There will be no wedding night."

Her eyes flew up to his, and he couldn't ascertain what he saw in them – relief? Apprehension? Doubt?

"I see," was all she said, before returning her attention to her plate, and Benedict rolled his eyes. This was one of the many reasons he had decided not to marry – because women were a nuisance, they never knew their own minds, and they were far too difficult to understand. He had thought she would be happy about his revelation.

"I appreciate you having dinner with me tonight," she said, changing the subject as she dabbed her lips with her napkin. "However, I know that you had no wish to marry me, and you have no intention of spending much time with me. I understand if you have other dinner arrangements each night. I will always be here, however, if you care to join me. I also might invite other guests now and then."

"No."

"No to… joining me?"

"No to it all. Dinner together. Guests."

"But it would only be one of my sisters or—"

"I said no," he ground out. "I will have no one else in my house. No visitors. I do not care if it is your mother or sister or another long-lost sibling that you drag up. None of them will set foot in my house. You can go where you'd like, meet them wherever you want. But not here."

She blinked at him for a moment as though surprised at his outburst, before she shrugged her shoulders and said, "Very well."

It was his turn to stare at her in surprise.

"That's it?"

"What do you mean?"

"You accept that?"

"Do I have any choice?" she asked. "This is your house. If you do not want other people within it, then I must respect that."

He opened his mouth and then closed it again, finding he had no words to properly respond to her. It was like she didn't realize who she was dealing with, how much better off she would be if she avoided him completely.

"Where is my paper?" he said instead.

"Your paper?" she repeated, feigning innocence, and he eyed her with a look.

"The one you stole from me."

48

"It is no longer in my possession."

"You gave it to your brother then," he said, running a hand through his hair.

"My brother-in-law, actually."

"They will find nothing from it. And I will have lost information that I dearly needed."

"Information far more valuable than collecting on the debts owed to you?"

Her question surprised him, for it meant she understood more than he would have thought.

"I will collect. When the time is right."

He knew she hadn't gone far enough in his ledger book to fully understand the situation. For if she had, she would never be here. Once his plan went into action – the one in which he brought down the entire Remington family – she would be gone from his house as fast as she had snuck into it through the back window.

It was the second reason he had agreed to marry her. He knew it wouldn't be for long – and it didn't matter as he'd known he would never marry anyway.

Not anymore. Not after his last attempt, which had been ruined by the man he had thought could bring no further harm to his family. He had been wrong then. He never would be again.

"What do you do during the day?" she asked, changing the subject, and he looked up from his plate to meet her direct gaze. He didn't like the way she seemed to stare right through him, as though she could see his very soul.

"I work."

"On what?"

"On everything that requires my attention," he growled. "That is all you need to know."

"Very well."

"You?"

Why was he asking? He didn't care what she did during the day.

"I do a great deal. I have many interests. Tomorrow I will be leaving shortly after noon with a friend."

"Who?"

"Does it really matter to you?"

"No. But I should know who my wife is accompanying."

And whether the person's family owed him any amount of money.

"Hugo Conway."

"Hugo Conway?" How did he know that name? But it didn't matter. His wife was not going about with another man.

"Yes. He has been my friend since childhood."

"Is he married?"

"He is not." Why did she appear uneasy when she said it? A sinking dread began to grow within him – dread that there was much more to this friendship than she was letting on.

"Why didn't you marry *him*, then?"

Her gaze flew up to meet his, the single sign that his question disconcerted her — the clenching of her fingers around her wine glass.

"He and I are friends and will always be only friends."

"You and I are far less than that. Yet here we are," he noted, and she flinched.

"Perhaps. But… there are reasons he could not marry me. Reasons that are not mine to tell."

"He is in love with another?" Benedict prompted, and when she said nothing but flicked her gaze away, he knew he was right. "Well, I do not care. You are not to be seen with him."

For the first time, it seemed he had elicited a response from her, as her eyes rose to his in panic and she stopped chewing the green bean she had just stuffed into her mouth.

"Pardon me?"

"I said that you will not be seeing him again."

He wished that he could hide the rage that was beginning within him at the thought of her out with another man. But, whether or not he and his wife actually liked one another, were married in more than name, she was *his*, damnit, and he wasn't about to let another man have her.

The thought scared him for a moment, until he allowed the swell of his anger to overcome the fear that there might be another she loved, another who would have suited her far better than he did.

"What happened to your promise that we lead separate lives?" she asked, her eyes flashing as a red hue began to float up her neck and into her cheeks, the first sign that, despite her rather even tone, she was far from pleased.

"I believe you just made a promise to obey," he countered, knowing she was right but unable to keep from this current path of conversation, even though he knew it would lead nowhere except potentially over a cliff.

"As though you meant any of your marriage vows," she scoffed. "What was the first? To love me? Do you even know what love means?"

He thought he had. But every person he had ever loved had left him, one way or another. No one had ever loved him enough to choose him over whatever demon they were battling.

"Nothing good comes from love."

She pushed her plate to the side, both of them having given up any pretense of actually eating.

"Who hurt you?"

Everyone.

"I am not speaking of this further. Do not go out with another man."

She was silent, and he knew that the only reason she

wasn't arguing was because she had no intention of doing what he said.

"I mean it," he added, and if he wasn't mistaken, he saw the slightest of smirks dance over her lips.

"Or what will you do?" she asked, lifting an eyebrow, and he had suddenly had the maddest idea to kiss the words off her mouth.

"You do not want to know."

"Actually, I do."

Bollocks, she was impertinent.

"Do not push me, Prudence," he said, as he slid his chair back away from the table, refusing to wince at the loudness of the legs scraping over the floor.

He had to get out of here – and quickly – before he did something he would later regret.

He could feel her eyes on his back as he stormed out of the room, and he didn't like how after just one day she had already found a way under his skin.

He did not like it one bit.

CHAPTER 7

"hat could you have possibly expected?" Hugo asked as Prudence met him around the corner from the townhouse she now called home, gladly escaping its confines and the man it held within. Its interior was nearly as drab and grey as its owner.

Prudence had never been one to concern herself with the aesthetic around her, but even she knew she couldn't live for a great length of time in such melancholy. She would have to recruit her sister and sister-in-law to help her make some changes, once she established herself in the household. So far, the servants, as few as they were, had welcomed her, and Benedict hadn't *seemed* opposed to the idea of her updating some of the decor. Not that she was about to ask for any of his opinions.

Today, however, she had other things to do. Namely, practice at Angelo's without her husband discovering her secret or her whereabouts.

Not that he seemed to have any interest in her besides telling her what she was not allowed to do.

"I certainly did not expect him to place so many rules upon me," she said, finally answering Hugo's question. "Not see you? Can you imagine?"

"I do not agree with him, you know that, but I can also see his position. What man wants his wife running around with another gentleman? Whether or not he cares himself is one thing. He is likely more afraid of how it would look to the rest of society."

Which hurt more than she would ever admit, but she certainly couldn't tell Hugo that.

"He claims he doesn't care what society thinks of him."

"Many say they have no care for what others think, but they are all lying to themselves, at least a little bit."

"You are a wise man."

"I know," Hugo answered with ease, and they both laughed. "So, no wedding night you say?"

"No," Prudence said, sobering. "He told me at dinner that I should not worry, for one was not forthcoming. Would you know if he—er… does not prefer women?"

Hugo rubbed his thumb over his chin. "I likely would have at least heard rumors by this point, unless he has never outwardly portrayed any leanings of the sort."

Prudence nodded, unsure whether the answer caused her hope or dismay.

"As I thought," she said, hoping her words sounded as dismissive as she meant them to. "It is *me* that he has no attraction to."

Hugo eyed her as they reached his building, where she would change before continuing. "I highly doubt that his decision had anything to actually do with you, unless perhaps he thought that was what you wanted?"

"I do not believe he truly cares what anyone else wants."

"Then it has something to do with his own personal leanings."

"You do not understand," she said, blinking away the tears that threatened. "Men do not look at me that way."

"I am sure that isn't true."

"It is very true, Hugo," she said with a small sigh. "I would know."

He placed a hand on her back for a moment. "If a man does not see you for who you are, then he does not deserve you," he said softly, and she had to pause to swallow the lump in her throat. "Do you want your husband?" he asked her now, and Prudence stiffened at the question.

For the denial leaped to her lips. Of course she didn't want him – how could she? But before it could actually roll off her tongue, something stopped her. An innate reaction within that told her as much as she wanted to deny it, perhaps she *did* want something from him, for reasons that she could not altogether explain.

As always, Hugo seemed to understand, continuing to speak as they entered his home and he began to unfasten the buttons on the back of her gown.

"You do not necessarily have to *like* the man to still desire a connection with him, even if it is entirely physical," Hugo said. "That longing for touch can be powerful."

Prudence blew out the air she had been holding in her lungs.

"All I can do, however, is ignore it."

"That is your decision," he said as she stepped into Hugo's bedroom to change into her fencing clothes. She had felt it too much of a risk to keep and wear her men's clothing in her new home, even if she hid them and covered them with her dress, so she had asked Hugo to keep them here for her. "I forgot to tell you with all the excitement of your wedding that you have another decision to make."

"Oh?" she said with some dread.

"Last time I was at Angelo's, he mentioned another match between you and Lord Trundelle."

Heat rose through Prudence's body at the thought, although she wasn't sure what it signified – panic? Anger? An innate reaction, telling her that she must say no?

"I am not sure that is a good idea anymore," she said, biting her lip, glad that Hugo couldn't see her through the door as he waited silently for her to continue. "He knows my face much better now. Surely, he would recognize me this time."

"That is a fair point," Hugo said, and she heard his footsteps as he must have started to take small steps back and forth from one side to the other as he considered the dilemma. "Perhaps you would have to be masked."

"What reason would I give?"

"You injured your face and need a mask to protect yourself?" he suggested.

"That's not bad," she considered, emerging from the bedroom. "How long do I have to decide?"

"I am sure that Angelo will ask you about it today," he said. "But I would guess a week or two."

She nodded. "A fair bit of time to fake an injury, then."

"I am sure we can come up with something that would be both entertaining and helpful," he said before adding, "or, you could say no."

"I could," she said, but it was half-hearted, for they both knew the truth – she wouldn't say no. She couldn't, not the way she was built, with a competitive spirit that ensured she would stop at nothing until she won.

"You're a brave soul, Pru," he said with a smile that told her this was his way of saying that he was proud of her.

"Or a stupid one."

"And yet you continue to win," he said, winking at her as

they stepped through the doors of Angelo's. "Time to show what you can do once more."

*   *   *

BENEDICT ONLY LIKED one kind of caller – the kind who came to pay him what they owed.

He did not enjoy the kind that came and begged for him to have mercy on them.

He did not enjoy social visits.

And he most certainly did not enjoy the visit of a duke and a detective who were there to question him about evidence that had been outright stolen from him and had led to his acquirement of a wife he never wanted in the first place.

He very reluctantly stood when they entered his study, although he waited as long as possible to do so, not particularly keen on showing the duke the respect that he most certainly had not earned.

"Your Grace. Mr. Archibald," he said, gesturing to the seats in front of him, for he had no desire to remain standing across from them in a bid to see who could outlast the other for the entirety of their visit. "To what do I owe the pleasure?"

The detective snorted at his sarcasm, but the duke remained unaffected as he took his seat.

"We have questions for you regarding your dealings with Lord Dennison and my father."

Benedict sat back and studied him. "The dealings with Lord Dennison are my business, not yours," he said. "I will handle it with the new Lord Dennison."

"Except for the fact that you own the man's vowels because of my father."

"According to…"

"This ledger sheet," the detective said, placing it in front of him, and Benedict laughed outright – not because he was entertained, but because he wanted to irk these two who obviously thought they were made of some superior quality.

"Ah, the one that was stolen from me," he said, taking it off the table and tucking it into one of his desk drawers. "I had been hoping that it would have been returned to me earlier as it cost me my freedom, but I will take it a day late."

The duke smirked. "Not to worry. We have great recollection of all that it includes."

"Know all you want," Benedict said, becoming rather annoyed now. "I have done nothing criminal. I have only made smart business decisions."

"Like it or not, we are family now," the duke said in an even tone. "My sister married you with the understanding that you would be fair to her and that you would not be of any danger to her. If there ever comes a time that I fear for her safety, I will have her out of this house as quickly as I can."

Benedict snorted. "Are you threatening me?"

"I am telling you the truth of the matter."

"Next time you threaten me, try choosing a consequence that I would actually care about."

The duke's face darkened, and Benedict congratulated himself on finally getting a rise out of the man.

"Where is my sister at the moment?" the duke asked, and Benedict shrugged nonchalantly, even though he found himself wondering the same thing.

"I have no idea. I told her she could live her life, and living her life she is."

"Is she unchaperoned?"

"She is a married woman now. She can come and go as

she pleases. I believe that was part of the reason she agreed to this sham of a marriage."

The duke shared a look with the detective then, and Benedict found himself surprised that he was actually enjoying this exchange.

"We overheard quite an interesting conversation between you and Lord Dennison not particularly long ago, and you did not seem to have a great deal of good will toward my family. I ask you now, as *part* of our family, whether any of us like it or not, to tell us the truth – do you know anything about who might be threatening us?"

"I do not," he said, holding the duke's gaze. For it was true. As much as he despised the Remingtons and had his own plans to bring about their ruin, he had no wish to see any of them physically injured, nor had he any idea of who else might want to cause them harm.

"Very well," the duke finally said, after holding his stare for another few moments in a silent contest. "If you ever have any reason to believe there is a threat to Prudence or the family, please do let us know. I know Prudence is a married woman, but I still fear for her safety. Archibald here will have a man follow her—"

"No."

"Pardon me?"

"Prudence is now my wife, and I will see to her comings and goings and safety. I do not need you or your dog."

"Now, see here," the detective said, his face darkening in anger as he began to rise toward Benedict, but the duke placed a hand on his shoulder to hold him back.

"Do not allow him to rile you, Archibald. He's not worth it."

The detective glared for another moment before he nodded as he pulled down his jacket.

"This has been such a pleasant chat," the duke said wryly.

"Please tell Prudence we hope she is well and we will see her soon."

Benedict nodded, but he doubted he would do so. For that would involve talking to Prudence again.

And he had decided that was not something he would do anytime soon.

CHAPTER 8

*B*enedict did not enjoy the fact that he found himself checking the time over and again – to see if Prudence had returned home.

As he stared at his mantel clock in annoyance that he seemed to care when she arrived, he heard the door open and he busied himself again, knowing that no one else would be calling upon them at this hour – as long as Prudence had kept her word, as she had assured him she was wont to do.

He didn't know if he quite believed her – at least not yet. She had to prove herself first. Everyone did, to him.

Benedict knew he should keep his ass exactly where it was planted, to continue to prove to his wife that he had no desire to learn more about her comings and goings nor her whereabouts.

Which was why no one could be more disappointed than he was with himself when he found himself standing and walking to the door of his study, peering out and watching her as she entered.

At first, he couldn't put his finger on what was bothering him, until he realized that she appeared rather dishevelled. It wasn't completely noticeable – a few loose hairs around her face, wrinkles in her dress that he knew her maid would have ensured weren't there prior to her leaving, a slightly askew bodice.

He reminded himself that he wasn't going to speak with her, that it would be better for both of them if he did as he said and lived separately. But he found himself speaking before he could stop himself.

"Have a good time?" he called out across the drawing room, and she jumped.

"Benedict," she said, placing a hand over her heart. "I didn't see you there."

"So it appears."

He began stalking across the room toward her, not taking his eyes off her as he did. Did she truly think she could allow him to be cuckolded like this?

His butler seemed to sense his mood, for he quickly made himself scarce from the room, waving away the maid who had arrived to attend to Prudence, leaving just the two of them alone together. Prudence maintained her position at the door, not walking toward him but not backing away either.

"I asked if you had a good time," he said in a measured voice, stopping a foot away from her, his eyes raking over her body from her head to her toes.

"I did, actually."

"Care to tell me where you were?" he asked, hoping the question sounded casual.

"Care to tell me about your every action?" she asked, fire in her eyes as she challenged him, and he hated the stirring between his legs at the spirit she possessed.

"I am your husband. I can ask you what I please."

"So much for the freedom to live our own lives," she said, placing her hands on her hips as she stared up at him. "You said you did not want to be married, that you did not want to have this commitment to another. Yet you seem to crave the power to control me. You cannot have it one way and not the other."

"According to whom?"

"To me," she said.

"Prudence," he said, stepping toward her, denying the fact that there was some truth to her words. "I am your husband. I can have whatever I want from you."

Even as he said the words, he knew there was no truth to them. He did much to evoke fear, but he would never actually force anything from her. He leaned down toward her, stopping a few inches away from her face. She wet her lips, and he found that as much as he told himself he must leave well enough alone, he couldn't help the fact that his body wasn't quite listening. The last thing he had planned upon was actually wanting his wife. For that would only lead to disaster, in more ways than one.

"What is it that you want, *my lord*?" she asked mockingly, even as she arched her hips slightly toward him and lifted her face to his.

"I want you to learn that I am your husband, that you must do as I say, and that if I ask you a question, you will answer it."

"Or else, what?" she asked, her challenge hanging in the air through the tense silence that surrounded them.

"Or I will take away all your freedoms. You will not have the opportunity to walk about alone. Just today, your brother and brother-in-law were here, threatening to have you followed to 'ensure your safety.' Is that what you want?"

He saw the fear in her eyes then, telling him what he had already suspected – she was up to something… or someone. And she didn't want her secrets to be revealed to anyone.

"I do not," she said.

"So I ask you again," he repeated. "Where were you today?"

"Having tea with a friend," she said. "Is that good enough for you?"

She lifted her chin defiantly, but he knew she was still lying. He had no idea, however, what to do about it. With everyone else in his life, he had power over their financial position or their status in society. He held nothing over Prudence.

It was then the realization hit him.

Between his own possessive wanting of her, the fact he held nothing over her, and her feisty spirit and determination to do as she pleased, he was in for a fair bit of trouble.

PRUDENCE WAS SUPPOSED to be determining whether Benedict was a threat to herself and her family. Instead, she was practically inviting him up to her bedroom.

So she decided to do what any rational person would do in such a situation – ignore him and hope that any desire she felt toward him would quickly fade.

She soon found herself tiptoeing around the house, attempting to leave and return almost silently so that he wouldn't catch her again. She had caught the suspicion in his eyes after the last time she had returned from Angelo's, and while she couldn't see how he could possibly know what she was doing, he obviously suspected she was up to something that he would object to.

She would have to make sure that he never discovered the truth.

In the meantime, Hugo had been right. Angelo had asked if she would face Benedict again, although he had not hidden his displeasure at how their last match had ended. Prudence agreed, already inventing reasons that could lead to a facial injury that would require protection.

She had been so invested in her imaginings that she had nearly missed the last bit of Angelo's suggestion.

"I am sorry, what was that?"

"Lord Trundelle would like to hold the match at his residence."

"Why?" she asked, taken aback. That would be quite the feat – leaving and returning from her own household.

Angelo shrugged. "He is not a man who often ventures into society, or so I am told."

"I did not think that he enjoyed having people in his residence."

Angelo looked at her strangely, and she realized there would be no reason for Mr. Peter Robertson to know such a thing.

"Apparently, he has made an exception for you."

With that conversation still lurking in her brain a few days later, she was surprised with what Jefferson greeted her upon her return that evening.

"This came for you, my lady," he said. "An invitation."

Prudence tore it open, eager to find what could be within, although she reminded herself that this was an invitation for Lady Trundelle and not for Mr. Robertson, so it could have nothing to do with what she was beginning to consider as something of a fencing career.

"An invitation to a ball," she said out loud, even though there was no one else in the room to speak to, unless there was a ghost or two lurking behind the heavy dark gold curtains. That was quite possible, as there were so many places to hide in this house with all the shadowy corners and heavy furniture. She tried to imagine Benedict living here as a youth, but it was difficult to see children within the walls. Had he grown up primarily at their country estate? She would have to ask, although that might lead to questions on just when they would be leaving to the country, which she didn't want to consider. She was lonely enough here in the townhouse when she could still visit her family. What would she do alone in the country?

As for this house, she wouldn't mind at least opening a few curtains, but when she had tried, Jefferson had been quick to tell her that Lord Trundelle preferred they remained closed. Of course he would.

"Where is it?"

Prudence jumped, whirling around to find Benedict standing in the doorframe. She had been too loud this time. She swallowed hard as she tried not to look at him too closely.

He made an imposing figure – she was unsure how much of it was on purpose and how much was his usual countenance. His dark hair was slightly too long, worn low over his forehead, while his dark eyes always seemed to be hiding exactly what he was thinking. She could never be sure of his true opinion on something.

Today he wore, as he often did at home, just his linen shirt tucked into his breeches. His golden skin was visible through the top of the shirt, and she wondered what it would feel like under her fingertips.

Now where had *that* thought come from?

This was why it was better that she simply avoid him.

He stared at her in silence as all those thoughts ran through her head, until finally she cleared her throat.

"Where is what?"

"The ball."

Goodness, how long had he been standing there? She looked down at the note in her hand, for it appeared that she needed a prompt to recall the sender of the invitation.

"Lord and Lady Waldenford's residence."

"Will you appear?" he asked, nonchalance in his voice.

"It is addressed to both of us."

"I will not be attending," he announced flatly. "I do not attend balls."

"You were at my family's last ball," she said.

He lifted a brow. "Notice me, did you?"

She didn't respond, for the truth was she had only known he was there because her brother and half-brother had overheard him in a rather suspicious conversation with Lord Dennison.

"I had business dealings," he finally said.

"Seems an odd place for them," she said. "Do you not think it wise that we attend an event together? We have not been seen together at all, and you know there is still a fair bit of talk about how we ended up married."

"A situation which was none of my doing and all yours."

A fair bit of guilt climbed over her as she knew that he was right. She was the one who had broken into his house, who had stolen from him, who had let herself into his study and made herself at home behind his desk. All he had done was enter a room in his own home.

But it was not within her to admit defeat.

"Whose hand was down my bodice?"

His eyes flared to life as he looked up at her.

"I was after my own possession, not anything you had to offer."

That was a bit of a blow to her self-confidence, although she wasn't about to tell him that. She knew she didn't have a particularly ample bosom, but surely it wasn't so non-existent that he didn't even notice it?

"No point in arguing," she said succinctly. "That is all in the past, and we cannot change it now."

"No, we cannot," he said, turning away from her, shadows

covering his face, hiding whatever he was feeling. "Go if you want. I do not care."

"Are you sure you do not want to attend?" she asked one more time, unable to help her guilt, as ridiculous as it was, about leaving him here alone. "I'm sure your brother and his wife will be there. I would very much like to meet them as your wife."

"You met them already. That is what led us here."

Clearly, he was in no mood to discuss this any further with her. His footsteps began to fade down the hallway, and she let them go, realizing with a sinking heart that this was the marriage she had agreed to, the only one she would likely ever have.

And that thought was more disappointing than she would ever have considered.

CHAPTER 9

*P*rudence knew she was not the most social of women, but she was looking forward to seeing her family and spending time with other people. She hadn't realized until she arrived at the ball just how lonely she had become at Benedict's house – she still had a difficult time considering that the townhouse was now *her* home as well. It certainly didn't feel like it yet. She wondered if it ever would.

"Prudence!" Emma greeted her with some excitement. Juliana and Maria, with whom she would previously also spend most of her time in these circumstances, were not in attendance, seeing as how they had both married men who would not be invited in such circles – Juliana to the detective Matthew Archibald, and Maria to Prudence's half-brother, the physician Hudson Lewis. While the Remington family had accepted him privately, Hudson had no wish to make his parentage known, and they respected his decision, especially knowing that the *ton* would not make it easy for him within their circles, even though he had done nothing wrong.

"I am so glad to see you," Emma continued.

"And you," she said, greeting her sister-in-law warmly.

Emma may always have been Juliana's closest friend, but by nature of her frequent presence at Warwick House in London and Remington Manor in the country since they were children, Prudence knew her nearly as well as her own sister. "How is baby Grace?" she asked.

"Wonderful," Emma sighed. "I am glad she is finally here, although I still worry."

"Because of all that still threatens us?"

"I am sure I would find much to worry over anyway, but of course, that has not helped anything." She linked her arm through Prudence's. "We can do nothing, however, but continue on as best we can, correct? At least you are able to look after yourself."

"I can certainly try," Prudence said with a laugh, "although I cannot carry my sword around with me."

Emma straightened. "Is that why your husband walks with a cane?"

"Does he?" Prudence asked, her eyes widening. "I have never noticed. He certainly doesn't at home."

"I am sure that he does," Emma said, tapping a finger against her lips. "Not that he is out very often – which probably makes his presence that much more noticeable when he does appear. But I swear he carries a cane."

"I shall have to check," Prudence said. "Perhaps I can borrow it."

They were both still chuckling at the thought when Giles joined them, passing Emma a drink.

"Prudence." He nodded. "Good to see you. Did your husband accompany you tonight?"

"He did not. Apparently, he prefers to remain at home than show his face in society."

Giles' face darkened. "Did you come alone, then?"

"I did. I have a driver and a footman awaiting me, of course, but one of the aspects I do enjoy about being a married woman is the fact that I can go where I please, when I please, without question."

"Your husband should be seeing to your safety," Giles said tersely.

"I can assure you, Giles, that I can fend for myself," she said.

They turned then to watch the dancers swirling about the room. While Prudence had never been asked to dance often, she had always enjoyed the odd dance when she had the opportunity. She found the footwork a great deal like fencing, though she never told anyone that in her mind she preferred to consider her partner an opponent. Perhaps that was part of the reason no one ever wanted to dance with her.

"Prudence. You look well."

"Good evening, Grandmother," Prudence said, turning with a smile. "As do you."

Her grandmother waved her cane at her. "I look the same every time you see me. No need to pretend otherwise."

"I would never lie to you. You know that."

"I suppose I do," her grandmother said begrudgingly. "Where is that husband of yours?"

"At home. Marriage has not changed his preferences."

"I see," her grandmother said, and Prudence could tell that she wanted to say more but refrained. Prudence was glad. For she had a feeling that she knew exactly what her grandmother thought of the marriage, but she didn't want to hear any opposing thoughts now, not when it was too late to do anything about it.

"How is Mr. Robertson?" her grandmother asked in a low voice, and Prudence didn't rein in her smile. She had never told her grandmother about her fencing identity, but somehow her grandmother seemed to know all about it anyway.

"Mr. Robertson is doing quite well," she said. "He is

making a name for himself, despite his youth and size. Angelo says that he possesses a talent he has rarely seen among someone that young."

"I am proud of him, even if he did learn most of his skills from his father," her grandmother said. While Prudence's father had not made many friends for himself, she wondered if anyone had hated him nearly as much as her grandmother. "If there was one thing the Duke of Warwick ever did right, it was train Mr. Robertson despite all the reasons that he shouldn't have."

"As it turned out, there was one thing he did truly care about, besides himself," Prudence murmured, to which her grandmother nodded, both of them aware it was fencing he had loved and not his daughter.

"You should be out dancing."

"I would need to be asked."

"They are all too scared to ask you."

"Too scared?" Prudence repeated, turning to her grandmother. "Why would they be too scared?"

"Because of your husband," her grandmother said as though Prudence was a fool for not realizing it. "None want to cross him for fear of what he might do to them. He ruins men who slight him."

"Oh," Prudence said, feeling a fool. She had known he was into some nefarious dealings, but she hadn't realized the extent of it. "That is… unfortunate."

Her grandmother snorted. "You do not know what to do with this marriage of yours, do you?"

"Not entirely," Prudence admitted. "Not yet."

"Well, you are a smart girl. You'll figure it out eventually," her grandmother said. "I best be finding a chair. Standing here watching all these idiots falsely smiling at one another is hurting these old bones."

"I'll help you."

"Please do not. I am not completely done for yet," her grandmother said, and Prudence nodded as she watched her grandmother wander over to one of the chairs bordering the dance floor, although she didn't look the least bit fatigued.

"Is she gone?" Prudence turned to find her cousin, Lord Hemingway, at her side, and she laughed at him.

"Are you frightened of my grandmother as well?"

"No."

"You are," she said, but then looked around. "Not to worry, so are most people. Were you with Giles?"

"I was," he confirmed. "But I am now here to escort you in to dinner."

"Do not worry about me," Prudence said, waving a hand in the air. Their cousin – in actual fact, the son of their father's cousin – was a pleasant enough man yet she couldn't help but consider him rather a bore. She could hardly believe that Juliana had nearly married him. "I shall be just fine."

"I am not worried, but it seems that we are both in need of a dinner companion," he countered. "Now, come."

Seeing no way to refuse him, Prudence took his proffered arm, and they began to walk across the floor, just as there was a low rumble, although from where, Prudence wasn't certain. She looked up at her cousin. "Lord Hemingway, what is—"

It was then that a twinkling light caught her eye from above them, and she saw that the huge, exquisite chandelier, with all its candles and all its twinkling mirrors and gems, was dancing – and not in any way that made sense. It was swinging from side to side and was going to come down on them.

"Run!" she cried but found only an empty space beside her now as she heard the snap from above and crystals and candles began to rain down – trapping her underneath.

* * *

BENEDICT HAD TRIED to talk himself out of this fifty times as he had made his way here. He had walked, as his only driver had conveyed Prudence with the carriage. One didn't need multiple drivers when one lived alone and never went anywhere.

Fortunately, the Waldenford residence wasn't far, but it had given him ample time to consider his marriage and why he cared so much about his wife's actions, especially when the very reason he had agreed to marry her was with the idea that they would stay out of each other's way.

But he had been sitting there in his study, unable to concentrate on anything except what she was doing and who she was doing it with. He still had his suspicions about who she went out to meet each night, and he had tried to learn more about this Hugo Conway. But so far, he had come up empty of any reason to believe that the man had intentions toward his wife. He told himself that his concern had to do with the fact that if she found herself with child, he would still be considered the father, and he wanted nothing to do with that. He cared nothing at all for whether or not she, his wife, was in the arms of another man. For he cared nothing at all for her. Or so he told himself.

Perhaps he could find out more if he watched her tonight.

And so he had stolen out into the darkness of night, intent on discovering what she was up to.

He had arrived long after the time when the hosts would be greeting their guests, which allowed him to slip into the crowded ballroom practically unnoticed. He nearly recoiled at the crush of people around him, which quickly reminded him why he abhorred and avoided events such as these. There were so many people, none of them genuine, all saying exactly what they thought each other wanted to hear, before turning around and conversing about one another behind their backs. It was everything he despised about society.

Besides that, half of them hated him for they had either already paid him or owed him a great deal of their money.

He endured a few of their glares, but he cared nothing about that as he looked around the room for the one person whose actions he did care about. Not because she mattered, of course, but because she might bring shame upon him and the name he was diligently attempting to rebuild.

"There she is," he murmured as he saw her standing on the side of the dance floor, speaking to her grandmother. He hadn't seen her before she had left, but now he couldn't keep his eyes off her slender neck, which he could see from across the room beneath the upsweep of her hair, above the crimson of her dress. He hadn't known her to wear much color, but it seemed she had made an exception for tonight. He kept to the shadows, circling the room to get closer to her, but was stopped by a hand on his shoulder. He whirled around, one hand on the hilt of his cane in defense but stopped when he saw who it was.

"At ease, brother," Martin said, his wife smiling brilliantly beside him, as though she was ever so pleased to see her brother-in-law. Why, Benedict had no idea. He had never been particularly kind to her. "I thought I was seeing things. I was just saying to Amelia, that man looks just like Benedict, but I am certain it would not be him at such an event. I was just about to turn away when I saw the cane and knew it must be you."

"It is me."

"Did your wife convince you to come, then?" Martin asked, to which Amelia added, "I am so looking forward to meeting her again."

"Last time wasn't enough for you?" Benedict growled out,

feeling a strange protectiveness to keep Prudence away from anyone else – even if it was his brother, who was harmless.

"It would be lovely to meet again under different circumstances," Amelia said with her usual ability to say the right thing in any situation.

"Very well," he said, turning around to find Prudence. He was here now. He had been noticed. He might as well accept his fate. "She was over there," he said pointing, frowning as he looked around the ballroom, annoyed by all the colors and people who made it difficult for him to find her once more.

"Perhaps she is going in to dinner," his brother said. "Ah yes, over there."

Benedict's head snapped up to where his brother pointed, and at first was surprised by the warming of his heart when he caught sight of her. The feeling quickly faded to be replaced by an icy hardness when he saw she was arm in arm with another man. Then all thought and feeling fled entirely when he noticed something else – the chandelier above her. It looked as though – yes it was. It was falling. And Prudence was right below it.

CHAPTER 10

*T*ime seemed to slow as Prudence told her feet to run before the chandelier crashed down upon her. But the kid slippers that she so despised wearing found no purchase on the smooth ballroom floor beneath them, and she slipped before she could move, rendering herself even more helpless. She could do nothing but cover her head and hope for the impossible when suddenly she was being jostled, pushed, and flung to the side.

She bit her lip, covering her scream as the chandelier landed with a resounding crash and breaking of glass across the ballroom floor. The sound seemed never ending, echoing across the room as the pieces rolled and chased after all the feet that were dancing away from them. Lord and Lady Waldenford's ballroom floor would be ruined, that was for certain.

But at least Prudence was alive... as far as she was aware.

She lowered her arms and looked up and around her to see who had come to her rescue. First, however, she noticed that all in the ballroom were staring at her and the chandelier, and she began to crawl backwards away from it on her arms and bottom and feet... until she ran into a solid body behind her.

She turned, blinking in shock when she saw who was next to her, staring at her with his brows furrowed in what appeared to be anger, but she supposed could have been concern.

"Benedict?"

"Are you all right?" he asked gruffly, leaning toward her and running his hands over her arms, her cheeks, her head, as though assessing for any damage. "Did you get hit?"

"No," she shook her head. "No, I am fine – thanks to you. You – you pushed me out of the way."

She said the statement in wonder, for she was still having a difficult time believing what had just happened.

"What are you doing here?" she asked, hearing the bewilderment in her tone.

He looked around them now, at the gathering crowd that was beginning to circle, and when she saw the panic in his eyes, she realized that there was more to why he did not attend such events. He didn't enjoy the people who populated them.

"Come," he said, holding his hand out and she placed hers in it, shocked by the connection she felt to him even through their gloves.

He helped her to her feet as they began to walk through the murmuring crowd until they met Giles and Emma, who were rushing toward them, along with their hosts.

"Oh, Prudence, we were just in for supper when we heard what had happened. Are you all right?" Emma asked, horror on her face, and Prudence quickly reassured her.

"I'm fine. Benedict pushed me out of the way."

Giles looked over at Prudence's husband with some surprise, and the two held a stare that apparently contained a great deal of meaning until Giles finally nodded at him slowly in what Prudence assumed was gratitude.

"Thank you," he said gruffly, holding out a hand, but Benedict stepped back, refusing to take it. Ah, that was more like him.

"No need to thank me. She's my wife."

"Still," Giles said, although he dropped his hand, "we should have Hudson check her for injuries."

"I can assure you, I am fine," Prudence said, wishing they would all leave her alone.

"You could still be shocked by the event," Giles said. "Meet us at Warwick House."

At that, he turned and led Emma out the door, and Prudence sighed as she looked up at Benedict with a shrug.

"I suppose we should go speak to them all anyway," she said. "This can hardly be a coincidence."

Benedict's face darkened, and Prudence had a sinking feeling that this was not going to lead to a favorable outcome for her and the freedom she so enjoyed.

Yet at the same time, she found herself wondering... what had Benedict been doing here? And how had he known to come to her rescue?

She wasn't sure if she should be entirely grateful or completely suspicious.

* * *

THEY HAD BEEN MARRIED for over two weeks now, and until this moment, Benedict had never sat alone with Prudence in such close quarters, unless one counted the first dinner they'd had together on their wedding night.

Now he remembered why he hadn't repeated the occurrence.

The panic that had filled him when he had seen her in

danger was the very reason he had refused to let anyone else close to him – because he didn't want to feel that way ever again. He had loved and lost before, and it was not something he had planned on repeating.

He didn't love Prudence – how could he, for he barely knew her – but when he had seen her standing underneath that chandelier, an instinctive protectiveness he hadn't know he possessed had overcome him. His body had moved before he could even contemplate what he was doing, and he had never been more astonished and relieved than when he had found her unharmed beside the chandelier as it had plummeted to the ground in a terrifying, echoing crash. When he had brushed off his jacket and trousers, he had found a few shards of glass trying to find their way through, but he thought he had rid himself of most of them.

He was more concerned about Prudence.

Most women would be in hysterics at this point. But here she sat, as though nothing untoward had happened.

Benedict wished he could better see her gown, but they were clouded in darkness in the dim light of the carriage. Instead, he had to do the next best thing. He removed his gloves and began running his hands over the soft muslin of her dress.

"What are you doing?" she asked, jumping at his touch.

"I am making sure that you are not about to be stuck with any pieces of glass."

"I didn't feel any," she said, shaking her head, although she didn't stop his hands from brushing over her body. "I believe you were between me and the chandelier. Thank you again for being there and for keeping me from harm."

He nodded, even though he wasn't sure she could see him, before he stopped when his finger snagged on something sharp.

He muttered softly as he felt the prick.

"Don't move," he said, reaching into his pocket for his handkerchief so that he wouldn't bloody her dress as he used his other hand to reach down and remove the shard.

"Did you hurt yourself?" she asked, leaning forward, but he placed a hand in front of her.

"Don't move," he repeated, only now he found that his hand was resting on her bosom, and he could feel her sharp intake of breath beneath it.

It took him longer than it should have to remove his hand, and he found that when he did, they were both breathing more heavily than before.

"As I thought. You had glass in your gown," he said gruffly. "There could be more. Sit back."

She finally did as he said, and he finished reviewing the rest of her dress, not finding anything else.

"You're fine."

"Thank you," she said softly, and he wondered if her breathiness had anything to do with him. As far as he knew, she despised him. And yet... there did seem to be this physical pull between them, even though he wasn't sure he could ever overcome the circumstances that had brought them together.

"Can I help with your finger?" she asked, concern in her voice.

"No," he answered gruffly, hardly needing her to worry over *him* after all that had occurred. "Just a small slice."

Ignoring him, she removed her own gloves and took his hand between hers, the warmth of them seeming to go directly to his heart.

Prudence pushed the handkerchief against his finger.

"Does that hurt?"

"No," he lied, and despite not being able to properly see her, he could feel her disbelieving look.

"Fine. It hurts slightly."

"Then you might have some glass in it," she said. "If Hudson is at my brother's house, we'll have him look at it."

"He is the physician?"

"Yes."

"I can take care of it myself."

"Do you do everything yourself?" she asked then, and he could see the tilt of her head as she studied him. "Or do you ever let anyone in?"

"You're here, are you not?"

"Only because you didn't have much choice in the matter," she said, and he could hear the smile in her words before she appeared to sober. "Are you still regretting all that happened?"

He could hear the anticipation in her voice, knew that his answer likely meant a great deal to her. The truth was, he didn't know how he felt anymore. Of course he would prefer to still be a single man, but if he had to choose a wife, he supposed there were a lot worse than Prudence.

"We shouldn't talk of it, Prudence. It happened, and now we live our lives as best we can."

"Of course," she said, placing his hand back in his lap and slipping hers away. He couldn't help but feel a sudden loss.

"We're here," she said as the carriage came to a halt in front of a fence that enclosed the largest mansion in all London – a mansion that belonged to a duke who was now his brother-in-law, although he knew he likely wouldn't be enjoying his hospitality for long. "We best get this over with."

The house was rather well lit for the hour, and Benedict nearly backed out of the drawing room when he saw how full it was. There was the duke and duchess, of course, as well as a man that strikingly resembled the duke, who had to be the illegitimate brother. Poor bastard, to find out he was related to such a man as the former Warwick. A beautiful blond woman who Benedict recognized as having been married to Dennison – for a brief time – was with him. The detective was there as well, along with his wife, Prudence's sister.

He was surprised to also see an older woman there, one who could only be Prudence's grandmother.

"We sent around a note to Hudson before we left the Waldenfords," the duke explained. "He was able to arrive quickly. Lord Trundelle, you may recall my brother, Hudson Lewis."

They nodded stiffly at one another.

"I've told Hudson what happened. How are you feeling now, Prudence?"

"I am perfectly fine," she said, taking a seat on the sofa, leaving the sole empty space the one next to her. Feeling rather awkward standing there yet equally as out of place sitting among these people, Benedict finally decided the least worst place for him was beside Prudence. "Benedict is hurt, however."

"I am not," Benedict said, waving away the physician's concern. "A small cut from glass, but it is nothing."

"We'll have a look in a minute," Lewis said, and when Benedict caught his gaze, he thought perhaps he saw a flicker of understanding pass over the physician's eyes. He understood, then, what it was to come into this family a stranger, to feel the unease that was currently flooding Benedict.

"If everyone is fine, then perhaps we should discuss what happened," the duke said, leading the conversation. "The last we saw you, Prudence, you were about to head in to dinner, and we didn't think that Trundelle was at the party."

"I wasn't," Benedict interjected. "I changed my mind and arrived late. I was walking over with my brother and his wife to find Prudence when I saw the chandelier begin to swing."

"What are the chances this was an accident?" Prudence's sister, Lady Juliana asked, and her husband replied.

"Normally I would say it would have to be an accident, for what is the possibility the chandelier would fall at the exact time Prudence was walking beneath it? But it seems too great a coincidence when considering everything else that has befallen the family."

"But that's just it – how could someone time it properly?" the duchess asked, leaning forward, and the detective sighed.

"I've been thinking of that myself. All I can think of is someone must have cut or loosened something on the chandelier before the party, then somehow – a slingshot, maybe? I'm not sure – arranged for it to fall at the exact time Prudence was walking beneath it."

"Someone would have to be watching her all night to ensure that would happen," the duke said, and silence reigned as the room filled with a tension that Benedict didn't completely understand – until he looked up and found the rest of them either staring at him or purposefully trying not to.

"Have I done something?" he growled out, not enjoying the accusatory looks aimed his way.

"You weren't supposed to be there," the duke said. "You only appeared when this accident befell Prudence. Why?"

"I told you," Benedict ground out, hating having to explain himself to anyone, particularly the Duke of Warwick. "I changed my mind and decided to attend."

"Did you speak to anyone else before the chandelier fell?" Archibald asked.

"My brother," Benedict muttered. "That's it."

"So no one knows exactly when you arrived?"

"No."

"I see."

"This is ridiculous," Prudence said, and Benedict found himself both grateful for her interjection as well as annoyed that his wife would have to stand up for him. Then he caught sight of her face, and realized that, worst of all, she appeared to be wearing a look of doubt herself, and it hurt worse than any of the others' did. "Benedict was the one who pushed me out of the way. I would have been cut to pieces by the chandelier had he not arrived when he did and was already moving toward me which kept me out of harm's way. I should hope none of you are accusing him of anything."

"Unless…" the duke began slowly, "he set it all up so he could play the hero."

Benedict snorted, pushing against the arm of the sofa to lift himself up.

"This conversation is ridiculous. I am done with it. If you would like to accuse me of something, just come out and say it."

"Very well," the duke said, rising as well and facing him, lifting his arms out to the side. "Did you or did you not arrange for the chandelier to fall?"

CHAPTER 11

This was getting worse by the minute.

Prudence could admit that she had as many doubts about Benedict as anyone did – that was how she had gotten herself into this mess of a marriage, after all – but it was one thing to suspect the man. It was quite another to sit here and accuse him of attempting to murder her to his face.

Prudence stood and placed her hand on Benedict's arm, but he shook her off, an action that did not appear to go unnoticed by her brother.

"Did it ever occur to you to consider the guilt of the man who was escorting her across the room, who mysteriously disappeared during the chaos?" Benedict snarled, and Prudence froze for a moment. For no, she hadn't. She felt foolish now for not stopping to consider it, but where *had* Lord Hemingway gone? One moment he had been there, his arm beneath her hand, and then when she had seen the chandelier wobbling and told him to run, he had apparently listened to her, for he was gone before she could even notice he had moved.

"I sent Hemingway to you," Giles said, and Prudence felt Benedict growl rather than actually hear him say anything.

"Why would you send another man to *my wife?*" he asked, the possessiveness in his words sending a shiver – not an unwelcome one – down her spine.

"You were not there, now, were you?" Giles said with challenge in his voice.

"It was a good thing I was, in the end."

"I'm sure it was a misunderstanding that Hemingway will soon clear up for us," Giles said, but before Benedict could respond, their attention was caught by a rapping on the floor, and he looked up to find that Prudence's grandmother was standing and staring at Giles with disdain on her face.

"Do not be an idiot, Giles. Hemingway has been too close to all this too many times to not consider that he likely has something to do with it."

"I thought the same," Archibald spoke up. "Especially when Juliana called things off with him."

"You never shared that with me," Giles said, crossing his arms over his chest, and Archibald shrugged.

"I figured that I should look into my suspicions first before bringing them to your attention, knowing how close you are with him. From what I could ascertain, however, he was seen elsewhere during the times when he would have been behind any attacks upon the family."

"Could he not have been working with someone else?" Hudson asked now, "or have hired someone to do the work for him?"

They all fell silent for a moment as they considered the possibility.

"We must be careful," Giles finally said. "For he is family. We cannot accuse him without cause."

"As you did Hudson, you mean?" Prudence interjected. "Or Benedict?"

"Prudence…" Giles said, a hint of warning in his tone.

"Well, it is true," she said, throwing her hands out to the side. "You had no issue there. Honestly, Giles, this isn't like you. I believe you are allowing the threat of it all get to you."

"Of course I am!" he burst out, as Emma placed a hand on his back in support, and Prudence noticed that he, at least, didn't shake her off as Benedict had done her. Giles might be acting an ass, but he still loved his wife and would do anything for her. If Prudence had to guess, that was what this and his accusations against men he should know better than to accuse was all about – his worry was overwhelming him to the point he simply wanted this all done with. "I am the head of this family, and not only must I keep you all safe, but my wife and child as well. How much longer are we supposed to live like this?"

The words rang through the air as they all considered what he said, each understanding him in their own way.

Archibald nodded. "My men are at the Waldenfords' inspecting the chandelier. Hopefully, they will be able to ascertain just how this accident came about."

"And who is behind it," Giles muttered, before turning to Prudence. "You are sure you are fine?"

"Yes."

"Would you – both of you – like to stay here for the night?" he asked gruffly in what Prudence was sure was supposed to be an apology, but before Prudence could even consider it, Benedict was shaking his head.

"No," he said. "I will take Prudence home."

Home. Prudence wasn't sure where to consider it. Benedict's house hadn't felt like home, but then… neither did this one anymore.

"I shall walk you out," Hudson said. "I'll take a look at that hand before you go."

Benedict opened his mouth, likely to argue, but Hudson was already shaking his head.

"I will not take no for an answer. If there is a shard of glass in there, it could fester."

Hudson was rather quiet and unassuming, but in medical matters, he was firm and thorough. Prudence respected that about him.

She said goodbye and goodnight to her family before they walked from the room, Hudson and Maria following them. They stopped in the small front parlor for Hudson to examine Benedict, using his tools to poke and prod Hudson's hand, while Maria drew Prudence to the side.

They had never been particularly close, for Maria had always been the envy of the rest of the young women of the *ton*, but Prudence had grown to rather like her, especially now that she was married to Hudson.

"Is everything all right between you and Lord Trundelle?" Maria asked quietly, her eyes flicking over Prudence's face as though she was trying to get a true read. "I know he was friends with Lord Dennison, which will always leave me with suspicions about him."

Prudence glanced over to find Benedict's eyes on her, and she lowered her voice, even though they were standing across the room.

"I believe they were close more for business reasons that any other," she said. "I do not believe that Benedict was particularly fond of Lord Dennison, actually. I am still, however, trying to learn more about why and how they were acquainted."

Maria nodded. "If you ever do need anything and do not feel that you can go to Giles, please know that I am here for you – as is Hudson."

"Thank you," Prudence said, reaching out and giving Maria's hands a quick squeeze. She knew that Maria truly meant what she said, that she had a kind heart and was only trying to ensure that no one ever faced the same threat in her marriage as she'd had to her first time around. "I shall be fine."

"You always say that," Maria admonished, "but everyone needs help now and then."

Prudence felt tears prick the backs of her eyelids. She never asked for help – from anyone. She didn't need it.

She had always been just fine on her own.

And she would continue to be.

Although even as she said it, she realized that she was guilty of the very same fault she had accused Benedict of. But she *had* to continue to look out for herself. What other choice was there?

For she knew, deep down, that while Benedict had shown up at the ball for her, it was not because he cared about her and wanted to be near.

It was because he couldn't shake his suspicions of her. And she wasn't about to share the truth. Not when he obviously had so many secrets of his own.

It was a trust that would likely never come between them. It made her sad to think about.

But it was the truth.

* * *

HEAVY SILENCE HUNG in the air between them on the carriage ride home.

Benedict had this strange longing to reach out and wrap Prudence in his arms, to ensure that she never came to any harm again.

But that, of course, was ridiculous.

She was his wife in name, but he had made it very clear that was all they were ever going to be. What he hadn't planned on was actually liking her. She had an independent spirit that appealed to him, was as afraid to ask for help as he was, although she likely would never admit it, and seemed to understand when she needed to push him and when to leave him alone.

In fact, the entire evening had him rather disconcerted. For he should have been sitting in that room hating every single person within it. They were the family who had caused his father's ruination, who had forced him to his death. Then Benedict had lost his mother to her grief, and he had been left alone, given the responsibility to look after Martin at an age when he had no business looking after another child, let alone a crumbling earldom.

All because of the Duke of Warwick.

He couldn't say that he particularly cared for the current duke, who was better known now as Remington, but he couldn't forget the conversation that had occurred as the physician, Remington's half-brother, a bastard, had tended to his hand.

"Do not take it personally," Lewis had murmured under his breath as he had treated Benedict's finger, much more delicately than Benedict would have done himself. As it turned out, the doctor was rather good at what he did and nothing like any of the physicians with whom Benedict was familiar.

"What's that?"

"Remington's accusation. He did the same to me not long ago. I hated him for it, wanted nothing to do with him or the family. When he realized his error later on, he did apologize. At first, I didn't accept, until I finally realized that Remington is only concerned with keeping his family safe. He has no idea where to turn anymore, or where any clues lead, and he is desperate."

"Desperate enough to accuse another member of the nobility?"

"Yes, absolutely," Lewis had said. "He shall realize his error once more soon enough."

"You truly believe me to be innocent?" Benedict had asked, so shocked that he didn't even notice the physician pull the tiny fragment of glass out of his finger.

"I do," Lewis said, smiling in grim satisfaction at his work. "For you would not look at Prudence the way you do if you were guilty."

Benedict started at that. "While I appreciate the support, I do not know what you could possibly mean."

Lewis just clapped him on the shoulder and turned him back toward his wife. "You'll learn in time," he had said. "Now, take your wife home. She does not appear to be requiring any recovery from her ordeal, but I would suggest that she try to get some rest in case she becomes over-whelmed once there are no longer so many distractions about."

Benedict was thinking over the man's words now as they drove. Prudence's scent filled him, making him suddenly wish that he was a different man, that they were leading different lives, that she was his wife in truth.

But it was not to be.

"I apologize for my brother," she said as the carriage came to a stop, and he reached out to help her down. "He should not have accused you like that."

"I would expect nothing less."

"He must not think you so bad, if he agreed to our marriage."

"Agreed?" Benedict snorted. "He orchestrated the entire thing."

"I do not suppose he felt he had much choice," she said

with a shrug. "But I believe a wise man told me recently that this is our truth now and we must move on regardless."

Benedict couldn't help but chuckle slightly as she threw his words back at him, although she had said them without any malice.

He led her into the house, Jefferson looking at them in some surprise when they entered together, likely because it was such a rare occurrence for them to be together.

Prudence placed her hand on the banister to go upstairs, pausing as she looked back at him, as though she was not certain what to say. The fact was, neither did he. He knew she likely expected him to retire to his study where he spent all his evenings, but he couldn't find it within himself to leave her. Just as he hadn't been able to help but follow her to the damn ball.

So instead, he placed his hand on her back to lead her up the stairs. But of course, Prudence being Prudence, instead of simply accepting the gesture of his assistance, she stared at him in surprise.

"What are you doing?"

"I am going upstairs."

"I assure you that I am fine."

"I know," was all he said as he began walking her forward, and this time she allowed him to lead her without protest.

He stopped in front of her door, knowing where her bedroom was, of course, though he had never gone within himself. He hesitated outside the threshold, not entirely sure what to do. He didn't want to give her the idea that he was waiting for an invitation, but neither did he want to continue walking.

He was caught between the man he was and the man he should be for Prudence.

And he had no idea what to do about it.

CHAPTER 12

*P*rudence's heart was racing as fast as if she was about to begin a fencing match.

She shouldn't want Benedict. He was not a good man.

Or so she had thought.

She was beginning to wonder if there was more to him than he showed the world, if he actually did care more than he ever let on.

"Why did you come tonight?" she asked suddenly, not even aware it was the question that was going to emerge from her mouth until she heard it herself.

"I explained why," he said, his expression darkening, as the space between them suddenly seemed far too crowded. "Because you were there."

"Yes, but why tonight? Why this ball? I go many places alone."

"Do you truly want to know?" he asked, stepping even closer toward her, invading the small space that remained between them.

She tipped her chin up defiantly, refusing to allow him to see that he affected her.

"I asked, did I not?" she challenged him, and she saw the fire flash within his gaze, although she wasn't sure whether it was in anger or desire. Though perhaps, for Benedict, the two went hand in hand.

"Very well," he said, reaching out and gripping her hips between his hands. "If you truly want to know, I came because I wanted to see you – and to determine what you are hiding from me. How you act without me. Whether there is another man you prefer to me."

His eyes had darkened as his hands tightened possessively on her hips, causing Prudence to gasp. She had known he had been suspicious of her, but never had she considered that he was jealous, thinking that she might be choosing another man over him. While she didn't enjoy the fact he would think such things of her, the intensity of his words caused a revelation within her.

"Why do you care?" she asked, tilting her head to the side as she wished she could see within his mind to what he was truly thinking. "I thought we were husband and wife in name only."

"Do what you please in every aspect except one," he said, his voice hoarse and his breathing ragged. "You will not enter another man's bed."

"It is not as though I am in yours," she retorted, not telling him the truth – that she had no intentions of being with any other man. Even though her marriage vows contained no aspect of love within them, she still intended to be true to them. For she didn't seem to have desire within her for any other man except for Benedict. Which was disconcerting in itself but not something that she seemed to have any control over.

He growled and before she knew what was happening, he was stepping forward with her, pushing her back against her door, his hands cushioning her as she crashed into it. His head dipped and his lips met hers, forcefully, hungrily, and while she knew she should push him away, that this was not how she wanted him, her body had ideas of its own as her hands wrapped around his neck and she kissed him back with equal eagerness and ferocity.

His tongue teased the seam of her lips, forcing entrance within, but she accepted him, enjoying all that this kiss had to offer, all that he was giving, as their frustration with one another came pouring out between them.

He was not the man she thought he was. But neither was he the man she had ever seen herself with.

He was something else entirely.

And he was her husband. A man from whom, at the moment, she desperately wanted more.

She reached back, fumbling behind her until she found the door handle, and when she opened it, they fell into the room together. She broke from the kiss to murmur his name, and his hands swept over her, holding her tightly against him, the bulge in his trousers pushing against her stomach.

"Here I thought you didn't want me," she said, her lips quirking up into a grin, and he paused as his hand snaked toward her bodice. "Are you trying to brand me for yourself? Keep the other men away?"

He backed up suddenly as if she had poured cold water over his head. His face was contorted in anger, until he ran a hand over it as though trying to hide his expression from her.

"Did I say something wrong?" she asked, uncertainty flooding through her now. Here she thought they were taking a step forward, but it appeared that there was more lurking behind that handsome face of his. She supposed she should have kept her mouth shut. It usually did get her into too much trouble.

He looked up at her then, meeting her gaze directly.

"There is something you need to understand."

"Very well," she said, placing her hands on her hips as she waited. Had she been wrong? Was it not what she said at all but rather that her kiss had been terrible, that he had no actual desire for her? Did he want nothing to do with her ever again?

"There is a reason I never want to see you with another man. It is not because I care if you are in his bed. It is because I do not want to produce any heirs. Thanks to Martin, the line will continue without me having to do anything to worry about it. If you were to get yourself carrying another man's child, the bastard would be considered mine regardless of whether or not I actually sired him. A child is something I do not need – or want – in my life."

Prudence blinked, having a hard time understanding what he was saying as the ferocity of his words overshadowed all else.

"I don't understand," she said softly. "Even if Martin has children who could continue the line, what does that have to do with any children of your own? You could have daughters. Or a son who could add to the line."

Daughters or sons who would be hers.

"No one needs a father like me," he bit out, and Prudence could only stare at him as the heat that accompanied the words left her chilled in its wake. There was obviously so much more he had left unsaid, so much that would explain why he felt the way he did.

But he was protecting himself by keeping it all from her.

"So what, then?" she said, flinging her hands out to the side, as unfulfilled longing and desperation flooded through her. She had known when she married him that it wouldn't be the life she would have otherwise chosen for herself, but she hadn't thought it would be like this – hurtful because now she knew him, and there was more to him than she ever would have previously considered. "I am supposed to spend the rest of my life with an empty bed, an empty heart, and no children to fill the void?"

His glare pierced through her, seeming to go right into her chest.

"I didn't ask for this. I didn't want a wife either. You should have chosen another home to break into like a thief."

And with that, he stormed out of the room, slamming the door behind him.

Leaving Prudence utterly shaken.

THE MOMENT he left her room, Benedict sank down in a low crouch against her door, his head in his hands.

He was the worst sort of man. He had told her that from the beginning, but how he had just treated her, what he had said and how he had said it, proved how very true that was.

She was everything any man could ever want, and he could have all of her if he truly wanted her. He wouldn't have thought that at the beginning of their marriage, but he could see in her eyes that she wasn't averse to him, that even if she was far from falling in love with him, she wanted him – physically. He could be in her bed right now, making love to her, proving to her that she was more than enough, that she was worth all the love in the world, that she didn't have to face everything by herself. He could be the one to stand up with her.

But instead, he had thrown all that was building between them back in her face by sharing some of his deepest and darkest secrets.

Any hope they'd had of coming to an understanding had fled.

He heard a choked sob from within the room, and, knowing that he was the cause of it and not the one who would be there to soothe her, he pushed away from the door and hurried down the stairs, nearly tripping in his haste to find his place of solace, where he could escape from the world and focus on the reparations he was slowly building.

He flung open the door of his study, closing it firmly behind him and placing his back against it as though by doing so he could avert all the demons that were chasing him.

Except even he knew that was an empty dream, for his demons were coming for him from within.

Benedict had been a man who firmly denied his feelings, who wanted only to act on what he knew to be true and what he could change. But here he was instead, with all sorts of conflicting emotions for his wife, emotions that he could no longer deny, that he wanted to run from as fast as he could.

Except he knew that wherever he went, they would follow.

And he had no idea what to do about it.

* * *

PRUDENCE ALLOWED herself a few minutes to wallow in self-pity for the marriage she found herself in.

And then she decided that she was not this woman. She was the woman who took charge of her life, who met any obstacles head on.

And her husband was most certainly an obstacle – to her, and to himself.

After she had allowed the sting of his words to subside, she had realized something. While he had been lashing out at her, he had also been telling her more about himself, his vulnerabilities, and why he was the man all perceived him to be.

He had a deep-seeded hurt within him. She knew it wasn't her responsibility to fix it, but who else could help him work through this? For what sort of man chose not to have children because he thought he wasn't worthy of them and their love?

She took a breath, facing her reflection in the mirror as she composed herself. He had been there for her tonight – physically, at least, until all turned sour – and had saved her life. She had no idea if he would allow her to help him in turn.

But she wouldn't be herself if she didn't at least try.

She knew where she would find him.

Her heart began to hammer with unease as she walked down the stairs toward him, but she knew that if she didn't attempt to mend this now, there might never be another time when she could possibly be able to solve all that was between them.

She lifted her fist, summoning all her courage as she knocked on the door.

She could hear him shuffling within. A few moments ticked by until he growled. "Come in."

Prudence opened the door, stepping into the lion's den before she shut it behind her, although she kept her back against it and didn't venture too far in for fear of being bitten.

"What are you doing?" he asked, his head bending low over his ledger book once more after he saw it was her standing in the doorway.

"I wanted to speak with you."

"Have we not said enough already?"

"No," she said, bravely beginning to take steps forward

toward him. "You said all that you wanted to say, but you did not give me a chance to respond."

"Perhaps there was a reason for that."

"Benedict." She stopped in front of his desk now, perching on the edge of it so that she could be near him and see his expression in the dim light of the room, which reminded her of the night they had been caught in here alone together, leading to their marriage. "There is obviously more to this than what you've told me."

"I assure you there is not."

"If you do not want to have children, then we can do all that we can to avoid it," she said, though even if he had been looking at her, she wouldn't have been able to meet his eye while discussing such a topic. "But before we make that decision, should we not speak about why you feel that way?"

"It has nothing to do with you."

"Actually, it does." She inhaled a breath. "I did not have the most wonderful father in the world. You must know that."

"I do."

"I know nothing about your own parents – although I would like to, if you would be inclined to share."

Surely, there must be factors from his past that had led to his feelings now about a family of his own.

"I am not."

"Very well. But have we not agreed that the past does not always define the future? That we can make a new path forward for ourselves? I do not want to see you lose everything that makes life worth living because you do not feel you are someone who deserves to be loved. Everyone is worthy of love."

"I *have* known love," he said in a low voice, almost to himself more than to her. "And I lost it."

Ah. Some of the pieces began to fall into place. He was

scared to lose again – whether that be losing the love of his children or... or someone else. Like his wife.

"A woman?" she asked softly, even though it caused a sudden pang in her chest to know that perhaps the reason he couldn't feel anything for her was because he still felt something for another.

"There was a woman, yes," he said, slamming his ledger book shut and placing his hands upon it, folded over one another as he looked up at her. "I cannot say that I loved her, but suffice it to say that in the end, when it was time to make a choice, she did not choose me."

"Have you ever thought perhaps that was for the best? That if she could not see your worth, it is a good thing you did not end up with her?"

"That's just it," he said, and when she looked closer, his eyes were haunted. "She did see my worth – or the lack of it. She made the best decision she could have. One that you, unfortunately, could not avoid. For that, I am sorry."

"Do not be," she said, taking a chance and reaching out to run her fingers along the side of his face, over the coarse stubble from his forehead to his jaw. He flinched, but he didn't back away. "Sometimes I think everything has worked out how it was supposed to."

She thought she had gotten through to him, but at her words, he jerked his face away from her touch, and Prudence sensed that he had been pushed far enough for one evening.

"If you ever need me, you know where to find me," she said, although she didn't elaborate on just how she would be available to him.

She placed her hand on the door handle and was about to pull it open when his voice stopped her.

"Prudence?"

"Yes?"

"I should not have said what I did to you earlier. Yes, you

did let yourself into my house. But this is not all entirely your fault. And I—I do not want you in the bed of another man for *any* reason."

She nodded, not trusting words to form around the lump in her throat.

And then she walked away, for at this point, there was nothing else she could do.

CHAPTER 13

*T*his was not how his marriage was supposed to play out.

He had only agreed to this because he had been supposed to marry in name, satisfy all the people who felt that he had ruined Prudence's reputation, protect his own family's name, and then go about with life as he always had.

Instead, Benedict was having to forcibly prevent himself from making love to his wife as she began to etch a space for herself in his life.

The worst part was, he didn't even think she was doing it on purpose.

He had known about the threat to the Remington family, of course, but he had brushed it off as more of a figment of their imaginations, a way to create attention for themselves, to seem more important in the eyes of the rest of the *ton*.

But now he had seen firsthand that there was more happening than he had originally believed, and he was on edge, wondering how to best protect a woman who seemed to believe that she could do a better job of it herself than anyone else could do for her.

What he needed to do first of all was to clear his mind.

And there was no better way than a fencing match to accomplish that.

Fortunately, two days after the ball that had left him and Prudence at odds with one another, he was scheduled to meet Mr. Peter Robertson once more. This time, he would not allow the man to get away with either forfeiting to him or besting him.

Benedict was going to come away the victor. He would make sure of it, for it was one of the few areas of his life that was still in his control.

It was why he had asked that the match be held in his home, so if nothing else, he would feel more comfortable, and could perhaps intimidate the young fencer.

His valet helped him prepare, saying nothing, for he had learned early on that Benedict was not the man to spend a great deal of time conversing with. While Benedict was not overly friendly with his staff, he was a fair employer. Which reminded him of something else he had to speak with Prudence about. She would likely want to hire additional servants, which she could do – within reason.

Although, overall, she did seem to be a reasonable woman.

Benedict set his cane to the side. The sword that resided within it was not the one he used for matches, but one that was much sharper, much more deadly – for it possessed one purpose – to ultimately be used when absolutely required to protect himself.

For until now, there was no one else in his life who needed protecting.

He heard the knock on the door that resounded through the townhouse, and only then did he take to the stairs to greet the man from a higher position. As he hit the landing, he wondered where Prudence was. He actually wouldn't mind if she saw that he had some prowess in the sport.

He almost asked Jefferson but stopped himself just in time. He couldn't be seen showing a preference for his wife, now, could he? It just might get back to her, and his staff would also think him to be going soft.

"Robertson," he said to the man as he entered, this time alone, without his companion, nor Angelo. "Did anyone accompany you?"

"I am alone today," the man said, his voice somewhat muffled behind the covering he wore over his face. "Figured we best meet one on one."

"Why the mask?" Benedict asked, crossing his arms over his chest. He didn't think it would be nearly as fair of a fight if the man couldn't see.

"Injured an eye and my nose. Best to keep it protected."

"I see," Benedict said, although it hardly made any sense to him. Perhaps the man was an eccentric. Benedict didn't overly care, as long as he wouldn't use it as an excuse. "You can still see well enough to fence?"

"I can."

"Very well. I have a room at the back of the house prepared for the match," he said. "You are sure you do not want a second?"

"Not today."

The man followed him back and Benedict suddenly wished that he had arranged for this at Angelo's, for it felt rather intimate, just him and this man he hardly knew, fencing one another in his private room.

But it was too late for that now.

"In here," he said, leading the man to what used to be a parlor but was now set up as his own private fencing room. He kept it closed off from the rest of his house, for this and his study were two places he usually kept for himself alone, except the maids now and again when cleaning was required.

The man followed him in, his neck craning as he was obviously taking in the room that Benedict knew not many households would contain.

"Are you ready?" Benedict asked, wanting to get right to it.

The man nodded, and Benedict approached the middle of the room.

When Robertson began the salute, he made three beats of his foot, two with the heel, and the third with his entire foot. He lifted his left hand to his hat, but only briefly lifted it off his head, allowing Benedict to catch sight of a dark head of hair that caused a niggling familiarity to tug at him, although he didn't have time to place it. He saluted back with his sword outstretched, not having time to continue this meaningless dance through all the stages.

"There are no spectators here," Benedict said. "Shall we begin?"

Robertson nodded and lifted his sword, but this time, instead of engaging in the fancy dance that Angelo taught, he copied Benedict's move of simply lifting his sword and stretching out his back hand, although he still possessed a graceful poise that Benedict had seen in very few opponents.

Robertson quickly thrust with three motions of the wrist, his arm straight, his sword reaching toward Benedict's breast as he stepped forward toward him. He had the sword lifted in line with his temple to prevent a counter thrust before he recovered to the guard, the sword in a straight line toward Benedict. It was a strong move, and one that Benedict often used himself.

Which meant he knew how to parry it.

He recovered quickly until their swords tangled again, and as they were engaged in carte, the points downward,

Benedict lunged forward, plunging his sword under the man's elbow to his flank, turning his wrist upward to create an angle from his wrist to the point of his sword. He dropped his left hand under his right to avoid being hit as he thrust, although his opponent parried him again.

Benedict frowned, for it was a move that always worked, at least for him. He decided to step up the intensity as he threw his body back into a straight line, allowing Robertson four inches to the left of his sword. When his opponent made his move, Benedict pointed his blade in line with the man's breast in his quick parry.

It seemed to be the opening they each needed as they began to attack and counter in quick, strong movements. Unlike their first match, which had been a game of wait and parry, now they were both the aggressors. Benedict knew, deep within, that he was taking out all his frustrations from his relationship with Prudence and his inability to control his own life and throwing it into the match, but that was nothing Robertson needed to know.

Especially since it seemed the man had demons of his own to battle.

They were engaged in a dance of thrust, parry, retreat, and attack once more, until Benedict was sweating and breathing hard. There was no one to keep score, no one to impress, and instead of counting their points, it seemed that they were each going for a final victory. Benedict had no intention of hurting the man, but nor was he going to quit until he had him exactly where he wanted him.

Then Robertson lunged forward so quickly that his cap flew off to the ground before him. He jumped backward, away from the point of Benedict's sword, as his hand flew to his head.

"May we take a break?" Robertson asked, and Benedict growled "no," as he leaped forward to thrust his sword again.

Robertson parried just in time to protect himself, and Benedict grinned in solemn satisfaction as he realized that he had the man trapped.

Then a lock of hair sprang free from the man's queue, curling around his face in a manner that reminded him of someone else. Someone he knew far too well. Someone who—

"Aha!" Robertson took advantage of his momentary lack of focus and leaped forward, his sword outstretched toward Benedict, who was able to counter him at the last possible moment.

But now he had a new intention. He needed to know this man's identity. His true identity. For Benedict did not know of a Mr. Peter Robertson outside of fencing circles. But he recognized this man. He was sure of it.

He advanced on him now, causing Robertson to retreat, as though he sensed the change in Benedict's purpose. Benedict lifted his sword, only now, instead of his usual attack, he had a new aim – to remove the man's mask, to discover who was hiding underneath. The last time they had faced off, something about the man had bothered him, but now his instinct of recognition was much stronger, and he was determined to discover the truth.

"Take off your mask," he demanded, but Robertson shook his head as they circled the room, Robertson moving backward while Benedict continued to advance toward him. Robertson was on the defense now, lifting his sword to counter Benedict's every move. Benedict couldn't help a cry of annoyance from escaping as he was foiled again and again, until finally he was able to advance Robertson forward far enough to trap him in a corner. The man looked from one way to the other, seeking escape, but found none. He threw down his sword and lifted his hands, leaving Benedict no choice but to halt his own attack.

"You win," Robertson said, but Benedict shook his head.

"Not good enough. Remove your mask."

Robertson shook his head furiously, as more of his hair escaped what had become a wild queue in the back. He tried to dodge around Benedict, but Benedict stopped him at the last moment, throwing out his hand to prevent his escape.

"I said stop."

Despite Robertson's struggle to free himself, in one fluid motion, Benedict was able to dislodge the man's mask as he prevented him from moving forward at the same time.

And as what was nothing more than a piece of fabric fluttered to the floor, Benedict's breath caught.

For those green eyes that were staring into his were eyes that he knew very well. Eyes that were haunting his every waking thought – and his sleeping ones too.

It was Prudence staring back at him.

CHAPTER 14

*P*rudence blinked back the tears of frustration that threatened as Benedict held her in his arms.

His grip was strong, firm – but far from loving. It was the grip a man would hold upon another when he felt he was under threat and had to protect himself.

This had all been a huge mistake.

She never should have come here as Peter Robertson.

She never should have agreed to take on Benedict in another match.

She never should have risked everything for which she had worked so hard.

Prudence squirmed once more, trying to free herself from his grasp, and this time, in his shock, he let her go, and she stumbled forward a few feet away as he gaped at her.

"What in the hell is going on here?" he finally growled out, and Prudence opened her mouth a few times, trying to find the right words to tell him what she had been doing, who she was, but nothing emerged.

"Were you him – the entire time?" he asked, pointing to the mask on the floor as if it held Robertson's identity within it. "What were you thinking? You could have been injured. You could have been taken advantage of. You could have—"

"Made a name for myself," she bit back. "It may not be my name in truth, but when a woman fences, it is simply for her own fun, and as a lady, I certainly never would have had the opportunity without complete ruination of both myself and my family. But as a man? Peter Robertson is well known for his ability. His skills are growing. Angelo believes in him. And more opportunities are opening up than I could ever have imagined."

"As a man? You are a fraud," he said, his hands lifting out to the side.

"In what way?" she asked, knowing she shouldn't be surprised that he would disapprove of her actions, but still disappointed that the first person besides Hugo and her grandmother would have so little faith in her. "No one would ever take me seriously if they knew I was a woman. I know there are women who fence, but most of them are actresses and the like, and it wouldn't be a fair match. I am *good*, Benedict. You know I am. I would have beaten you last time."

"You would not have," he said, but she could tell that he didn't truly believe his own words.

"I would have, and you know it," she countered. "The single good thing my father ever did was teach me to fence. It was his favorite sport, and when Giles left the family, my father allowed me to continue to learn under him. It was more due to his love of the sport than any feeling for me, but once he passed, I knew the one way I could continue to improve was as a man. And so I did."

"All this time that you have been living here – as my wife – you have been fencing?" he said, his eyes narrowing, and she nodded.

"I have," she said, straightening her shoulders. "And I will not apologize for it. We agreed when we married that I could live as I please. And so I have been. I haven't broken any of your rules. I have not been with another man. Your reputation remains intact."

"Until someone discovers your true identity."

"No one ever has before."

"I came close, didn't I?" Benedict said, advancing on her now. "When you forfeited the match."

"You nearly exposed the linen I wear beneath my shirt," she admitted, and his eyes flicked down to her chest.

"That is how you cover your breasts?"

"Yes. Not that they are ample to begin with."

"They are nothing to be ashamed of," he said, his voice dropping, and Prudence heard the change in his tone, wondering at it, even though she wasn't quite brave enough to ask him what he meant by that.

"You have chosen not to know," was what she muttered instead as she turned her head away.

"Doesn't mean that I do not have my own ideas."

That was just about enough for Prudence.

"You cannot have it every way you want," she snapped, advancing on him now with one finger held in front of her, pointed at him. "You cannot tell me that I am your wife in name, that you will not come to my bed, that I am not allowed to have any children of my own because they will be yours, that we are to live separate lives as we choose, *and* that I am not allowed to do the one thing that I love, the only thing that brings me joy."

"Fencing?"

"Yes!" she exclaimed, wishing she could pick up her sword again to defend herself.

When he spoke, his voice was so low that she nearly didn't hear him.

"I never said that you couldn't fence."

"Pardon me?"

"I never said that you couldn't fence," he said, much louder now. "Go ahead and do as you please."

"I—" Prudence had been ready to argue with him again, until she realized what he was saying. "You do not care that I continue?"

"I am concerned for your safety, and for someone discovering your identity. But…" He ran a hand through his hair. "…I understand how much it means to be able to fence, and I would never take that away from you."

He looked away from her, as though it was too much to meet her eye.

"Thank you," she said softly, understanding what it meant for him to allow her that, and not sure how to properly say it to him. "I appreciate that."

"I do have a question."

"Yes?"

"What of Hugo Conway? He was with you the first time I faced you."

Prudence paused. She didn't want him to blame Hugo for anything, but neither could she ever reveal his secret.

"Hugo is a friend," she said quietly, entreating him with her gaze to believe her. "A good friend. But nothing more. You do not need to worry about him."

"How could a man be so close to you and not want more from you?"

"I cannot explain that to you, but just know that there is nothing to ever fear of what he and I are to each other."

He held her gaze for a moment then, until his brows lifted.

"He doesn't like women," he said, realizing the truth, but Prudence shook her head desperately.

"I never said that."

"You do not have to," Benedict said. "It makes sense."

Prudence blinked furiously as guilt began to seep down

her throat and into her gut. She had just ultimately betrayed the best friend she had in the world. Benedict may be her husband, but there was no way she could trust him.

"I will not say anything to anyone," he said, reading her mind, and when she eyed him, he chuckled lowly. "That will be easy, for I do not speak to anyone."

She found herself laughing a bit with him at that, and soon enough they were doing what she had thought was impossible– they were sharing a smile.

"I know you do not think much of me," he said gruffly. "But I do want the best for you, Prudence, truly I do. I know that might be difficult married to a man like me, but—"

She stepped toward him and raised a finger to his lips as his sword fell away from his fingers and clattered to the ground beside him – but neither of them made a move to pick it up or were even startled by the sound.

"You can be enough, Benedict," she said. "Truly you can. You just need to believe it yourself."

Then, before she could second guess herself and what she was doing, she stood on her toes, leaned in toward him, and touched her lips against his.

* * *

THIS WAS A MISTAKE. Benedict knew it the second the soft plushness of her lips met his, but then, when had a mistake ever felt so damn good before? He was more conflicted than he would ever admit, as the moment he had triumphantly uncovered Peter Robertson's identity, he had instantly been completely taken off guard and uncertain exactly how he felt about his wife being the man he had been facing off against, the man who had the world fooled.

This was no young phenomenon. This was a woman who was as good as she was due to years of practicing, with a man who all had hated – who *Benedict* had hated, with all his very soul.

And yet, he couldn't help but admire her for the lengths she had stretched to in order to achieve her dreams, even if that had meant lying to him and everyone else. She was a woman unlike any other, and she was his – in the eyes of the law and the church, at least.

So why not take her in this way as well? She was his wife, and she seemed to be equally as interested in and attracted to him as he was in her. He wouldn't do anything that would lead to a child, he promised himself. But she had started this – he might as well show her how things ended when she did so.

It was obvious that she was not overly experienced in the art of seduction, but that was just fine with him. He would prefer that he was the one to teach her that as skilled a fencer as she was, she could use her body – and his – in other ways that would bring just as much pleasure.

Although the truth was, while he was no innocent man, he was also not particularly practiced himself.

He could feel Prudence's hesitation as she kissed him, and he was well aware of why – she was worried that he would pull away, reject her again.

That was one worry she needn't concern herself with. Not tonight.

He applied pressure himself, and it was enough encouragement for her to part her lips and he slid in his tongue, unleashing the passion that had been building between them as they had argued, suspected one another, held the trust at bay.

It had all culminated in this fencing match, one that he wasn't entirely sure who had won, unless, he considered, maybe with this ending they both would.

He slid his hand around her waist, surprised as he had

forgotten that she was wearing breeches and not a dress, but that only made him want her more, for he could feel every curve of her bottom as he pulled her against him.

Her arms slid around him, one wrapping around his neck, the other around his back. The slight indent of her breasts pressed against his chest, but he damned the linen wrap she wore around them as he wanted to feel more – much more.

He left her mouth, his lips pressing kisses over her jaw, her neck. They were not chaste and sweet, but hungry, passionate in his need to taste her. He used his tongue, his lips, until he was nibbling at her earlobe and she moaned against him.

While he was aware of what they were doing, of course, Benedict wasn't quite prepared for when her hands ran down his body to the waistband of his breeches, before she slid one hand over the length of him; he groaned, arching in toward her. He took deep breaths as he tried to control himself, although it wasn't easy. He was to be the master in this, he reminded himself. Yet, as in the fencing ring and his home, she was proving herself to be as commanding as ever.

Here he had questioned how much she knew about what she was doing.

Well, two could play this game.

She wanted a match?

He needed to feel her – all of her. He stepped back slightly away from her and in one aggressive motion, he ripped the shirt up and over her head, eyeing the linen wrap around her chest with distaste.

"Get rid of this," he growled, and she blinked wide, glassy eyes at him.

"The linen?"

"Yes."

She worked at a clasp that held it together, and the

moment it was free, he lost control and yanked it from her to unwind it himself. Then, finally, it fell to the floor, freeing her, and he was like a man starved as he raised his hands to her breasts and cupped them as he lifted their weight in each of his hands, rubbing his thumbs over her nipples as she gave them to him.

She was right – they weren't ample. But they were the perfect fit for him.

He ran his eyes over her lean, toned body. Her shoulder muscles were sculpted from fencing, her arms strong and supple, and yet, she still possessed a femininity one couldn't deny. She was perfection.

He couldn't help himself now. He was grinding himself against her, even though the fabric of both of their breeches separated them. She stood on her toes, pressing into him, her arms around his neck, and he bent and lifted her legs so they were wrapped around his waist as he held her in his arms before backing her up until she was pressed against the wall.

His lips found hers and he made love to her mouth for a time that he never wanted to end before she tilted her head back away from him.

"Bedroom?" she asked, but he shook his head.

Yes, she was his wife, but she had entered this room as Mr. Peter Robertson. The last thing he needed was his servants telling everyone either that his wife was masquerading as a male fencing prodigy, or that he was tupping the man himself.

He had ensured, however, that every room in this house – particularly those where he found solace alone – were equipped with a lock, and he set her down long enough to walk over and slide it closed.

"Now," he said, stalking back toward her, "where were we?"

CHAPTER 15

rudence could hardly believe what was happening – to her.

Here she had thought that once Benedict had discovered her secret, he would be rid of her. Instead, it had seemed to do nothing but encourage him.

In the corner of the room was a floor covering that he obviously used for some sort of training. It seemed it was going to come in handy now as he laid her down upon it.

Prudence's breathing sped up as she realized what was coming – more than she had ever thought would be possible with her husband.

For not only was he now seemingly interested in making love to her, but he was doing so in a way that made her feel desired – like he wanted *her*, and not just any woman who came his way.

He knelt between her legs, and she wondered just what he was going to do with her breeches on until he reached up and with one quick flick of his fingers on the fastenings, they were open and he was tugging them down. She couldn't help but lift her hips to help him.

Prudence's throat went dry when she realized she was bare before him. Never before had she been so exposed in front of another person, and she had to fight against every inclination to close her legs and back away from him.

But he... he actually seemed as though he enjoyed what he was looking at, as he slid his hands up her legs, pressing her knees slightly apart. She took a breath, knowing that now was the time when he would push himself into her. Her mother had told her that her wedding night might be painful. Of course, her wedding night hadn't ended up being *physically* painful, but she had known what her mother meant.

Benedict's hands continued to trace light lines up and down her legs, his eyes hard as he looked at her like a predator would his prey.

"Do you recall your vow?"

"Which one?" she asked, hearing the breathiness in her voice but unable to do anything about it.

"The one to obey, of course."

"We discussed this already."

"Yes," he said, and finally, he smiled. She had hardly seen him smile before, and this one was rather wicked, but it sent shivers straight down to the very place he was currently staring.

Then his fingers replaced his gaze and Prudence forgot everything she had ever suspected of him.

She couldn't help the whimper that escaped when his fingers slid inside her, her back arching as she moaned for more. He moved in a rhythm, and then his thumb found a nub of sensation that nearly had her seeing stars.

"How are you doing that?" she gasped, and he chuckled lowly.

"Must you ask questions about everything?"

"Yes."

He removed his hands then, and she whimpered at the

loss of his touch – until he replaced his fingers with something else.

His mouth.

What was happening? How could he possibly—oh.

"That feels g-good," she managed to groan out, which was most certainly an understatement, but she found herself without the words to properly explain how she was feeling. Her legs fell even farther open of their own accord, and then he sucked her in a way she didn't know was possible and her hands gripped the blankets beneath her in an attempt to hang onto reality.

She was building toward something, something that was within her reach and that she needed with every ounce of her – then the ebb of ecstasy began to wash through her, and she couldn't help her cry, one that he reached up and prevented with his hand, as she belatedly realized that they didn't need the entire household staff listening to the two of them enjoying one another.

She had barely recovered when he was ordering her around once more, and while she normally would never put up with that, somehow, in this, she accepted.

"Do you trust me?" he said, and she looked into his eyes, knowing that in this, at least, she could. "Turn over," he murmured, and she drew a deep breath, unsure but knowing that if she did what he said, it would be likely be more than worth it if what had just occurred was any indication.

"On your knees."

She was doing what he was saying and not hating herself for it, which was shocking in itself.

"Are you sure you're ready?" he asked, and a small piece of her heart melted toward him because, despite the fact that she was his wife and he had every right to do this, he would ask her permission.

She nodded and then before she had time to think or worry, he thrust inside of her, letting out a groan of his own.

It certainly wasn't as painful as Prudence had been warned, although she wondered if part of that had to do with the fact that he had ensured she was ready for him.

He was more considerate than she had imagined.

Benedict stayed within her for a moment before taking hold of her hips and beginning to rock back and forth, until he suddenly stopped.

"What are you doing?" she cried out.

"This is going too fast."

"What do you mean?"

"I—oh, fuck, Prudence."

He reached around her, cupping one of her breasts as he began to thrust harder and faster against her, until she found herself building toward that place of ultimate passion again, and she cried out as it washed over her.

He thrust one more time, and then he was gone. When Prudence looked back over her shoulder to see what had become of him, he was running his fist up and down himself as he held a handkerchief beneath him, and she realized what he was doing. He had told her that he didn't want children. This was how he was preventing that from happening. And while she would never regret what they had just done together, she was equally as saddened by the thought that he was interested in nothing more with her.

She lay back against the mat before he caught her looking, for she had a feeling that would make everything worse.

When he was done, he said nothing, although she heard him walking around, collecting his clothing.

She wondered how much *he* regretted what they had just done. He had seemed interested, but now that he had finished himself, she wondered if he would have made the same choice again.

He went about dressing, and she watched him with narrowed eyes. If he thought he could ignore her and all that had just happened, he was sorely mistaken, and she was not about to sit here and allow him to do so.

He collected her clothing as well, passing it to her without looking her in the eye.

"Here," he grunted, and she lifted her eyes to him as she took it and stood so that they were at as equal stature as was possible.

"That's it?" she said, not allowing him to continue on without acknowledgement of what should have been a most magical moment together.

"What's it?"

"After what just happened, we just… get dressed and move on?"

He ran a hand through his hair, and for a brief moment, Prudence saw the vulnerability in his eyes and realized that the reason he hadn't said anything was likely because he had no idea what to say. But to be fair, neither did she, and yet here she was, willing to bridge the silence anyway.

"Did you enjoy yourself?" she asked, and that caused his head to snap up toward her with incredulity in his eyes, and despite all that she was feeling, she had to bite back a smile that she had shocked him.

"Now? Here?"

"No, when we were fencing." She rolled her eyes, trying to hide the fact that her heart was beating in a panic within her chest, worried that he had found her lacking, that she hadn't met with his expectations, that coming together had proven what he had thought and that this was never going to occur again between the two of them.

His face darkened at her sarcasm, and he turned from her as he picked up his sword and placed it within the rack on the wall.

"That should not have happened," he said, his voice growling.

"And why not?" she demanded as she finished buttoning her shirt and fastening her breeches, feeling that she could stand on equal footing with him now that she was dressed. "We are married. We wanted one another. Why should it not have happened?"

She did know why *she* shouldn't have done it. Because it left her open to him – open and vulnerable and wanting more. But since that obviously wasn't an issue for him, she wanted to hear just why he felt that a man should not make love to his wife – besides that he wanted to prevent children.

"Because we are hardly able to keep a marriage in name only if we are in bed together."

"Maybe we should be more than a marriage in name only," she said, stepping closer to him, physically feeling the pounding of her heart against her ribcage as she tried to shield herself from the rejection that was sure to come.

He was silent for a moment before he finally looked up, his jaw tense, his brow furrowed. "I can never give you what most women want."

"Which would be?"

"Intimacy. L-love."

Prudence ached slightly at the lack what could have been, but she would certainly never admit to him one of her deepest desires, one that she hadn't even been aware that she held within her.

"I do not need that."

He looked over at her with some skepticism.

"Are you certain?"

"Absolutely."

He shrugged. "Very well. If you want to be in my bed, then come in my bed. But do not expect anything else. Be sure to show yourself out as Mr. Robertson. Put the mask back on."

And with those words, he turned on his heel, and left.

Leaving Prudence staring after him, wondering what she had just agreed to, and why she couldn't seem to control herself when it came to him.

* * *

BENEDICT WAS RUNNING out of sacred spaces.

Every place he had previously considered a sanctuary was no longer available to him. His study had been his alone, but now, every time he entered, he was reminded of Prudence sitting behind his desk, her nose within his ledgers, her beautiful face lifting to meet his.

He hadn't wanted her there, and yet there she had been, causing a more abrupt and chaotic change to his life than he ever would have guessed.

The one other place that had been his and his alone had been his fencing room, where he had come any time he had something to get off his mind, knowing that by moving his body he could shake out his thoughts.

Now, of course, he would never be able to enter this room again without thinking of Prudence and what they had done together in here.

He had been a complete ass to her afterward, he knew that, even though she had been everything any man could ever have asked for, more than he would ever have expected from any woman, let alone his wife.

She had been passionate, accepting, eager, and he had never enjoyed a woman the way he had enjoyed her.

And then he had been aware that he had made her feel like she hadn't been enough. But he couldn't afford to give her any space – for if he did, she might find her way into places where he didn't want her, where he couldn't have her.

For this was all going to end. He had to continue to remind himself of that. He had made a promise – to himself, and more importantly, to his father's memory – that he was going to right all the wrongs that had been done to them.

It was all that he had worked for his entire life, and he couldn't sway from his path now.

In the meantime, he would allow himself to enjoy his wife. He just had to make sure that it stayed physical between them, that there was no chance she would find her way into his affections.

For that would be utter disaster.

CHAPTER 16

*P*rudence wasn't entirely sure how to greet Benedict the next day.

Fortunately, he solved that for her by being his usual surly self.

After he muttered good morning to her while he strode by her down the hall, she didn't see him until it was time for bed.

She had spent the entire day worried about what was to come, but that night, after her maid had left, Prudence looked up to find the door between their bedrooms was slightly ajar. Before, it had been not firmly shut but also locked – she had checked – so she wondered if, perhaps, this was an invitation. This was her marriage. She didn't have much choice in *who* she had married, but she was determined that she would try her best to at least find some civility, some common ground.

And then there was the fact that her body seemed to want him no matter how annoyingly grouchy he was.

In her nightclothes, she stepped up toward the door and pushed it slightly open.

Only to find Benedict within, clad in just his breeches as he lounged on the bed, his eyes hooded, his expression dark and hiding anything he might be thinking.

"Come in," he said, his voice so low it was nearly a growl, and she nodded slowly, her eyes on him as she refused to back away from his challenge.

While yesterday had been a passionate coming together, their fencing the foreplay, tonight had an entirely different air, for Prudence was aware that this was a choice they were making – and Benedict seemed to understand that just as she did.

He held her gaze as she walked toward his bed. The room was heavy, the curtains drawn and the canopy around the bed a navy blue so dark that it was rather disconcerting, for he was nearly lost in the shadows.

Prudence stopped at the foot of the wide, mahogany bed, but he made no move toward her. Had she been any other woman, she likely would have left for fear that it meant he wanted nothing to do with her.

But she was not a woman who ran. No, she was a woman who pursued what she wanted. And right now, with the aching between her legs as she skimmed her eyes over Benedict's hard, bare chest with its sprinkling of hair, she wanted *him*.

She unfastened the tie of her wrapper, allowing it to fall to the floor before she climbed up on the bed, her legs coming on each side of him as she sat astride him.

Finally, he moved, bringing his hands to her ankles before he began to slide her nightgown up her legs, over her hips, then across her torso until it was finally over her head and she sat there in front of him, neither of them speaking, just staring at one another.

Then he leaned up, wrapped a hand around the back of her head, and pulled her down toward him.

He was as aggressive as he had been the night before, his kiss hard and unrelenting, but she sank down into him, her hands splaying across his chest, digging into his skin as she kissed him back. This time, there was no intimate build up to the ultimate event. He stroked her a few times before he was unfastening his breeches, and as they fell open, she saw the hard length of him ready and waiting for her. He lifted her then, up over top of him, before he pulled her down on him and she gasped at how the angle allowed him to fill her.

His hands wrapped around her hips, and he began to rock her back and forth with a slight up and down until she found the rhythm herself. The slant had her rubbing against him in the very place she ached for him, until she found the now familiar and all-too-welcome pleasure begin to build within her, and when she began to pulse around him, she was slightly inhibited from fully enjoying the moment due to the pained expression that filled his face – until she realized why.

As soon as she began to come down from her own pleasure, he was lifting her up and off him, spending in a piece of linen beside him.

Prudence stayed where she was, sitting beside him exactly where he had left her, uncertain of what exactly she should do now. She had a feeling that they were not going to lie together on the bed and have a heart-to-heart.

As he had done before, he cleaned himself off and then pulled up his breeches, before looking up at her expectantly – and she realized he was waiting for her to leave.

"Do you need anything?" he asked, the first words spoken since she had arrived.

"I need—" Something. But what? All she knew was that she wanted more than this. More than this feeling that he had used her, even though she was aware that they had used one another in equal measure, that she had been a willing participant. "I'm fine," she said, turning her back to him as she threw her nightgown over her head, and then lifted her wrapper and tied it tightly as though it was armor that would protect her.

Her shoulders were stiff as she walked to the door, and she had just placed her hand on the knob to return to her room when he called out to her.

"Prudence."

She stopped, although she didn't turn around and look at him, for she didn't want him to see any hurt on her face that she might be unable to hide.

"We do not have to continue to do this."

She nodded. She knew they didn't have to, and yet, she had wanted this. She had asked for this.

"I know," she said. And even as she pushed through the door, she hated herself for knowing that, as difficult as it was to face such a man who kept everything from her but, apparently, his body now, she would be back.

* * *

THEY FELL into a rhythm over the next few weeks. They wouldn't see one another all day, and then night fell and Benedict would leave the door open to invite her in. Most nights, she accepted, and while Benedict could not have asked for anything more, he was also still unsure if this was the right decision. Their lovemaking was passionate, fulfilled all their desires, but he was determined not to provide her any emotional attachment. It wouldn't benefit either of them.

While she likely thought he was just being an ass, he was protecting her as much as he was protecting himself. He could just never explain to her why he was doing so.

Benedict caught sight of her most days leaving the house,

often dressed as Mr. Peter Robertson. She had told him to expect it, that she felt it was likely actually providing her the ability to walk the streets without notice or fear of threats that were still facing the Remingtons. There was truth in that, Benedict conceded. He had no idea what the servants thought of her attire, but he didn't overly care. If anyone discovered her identity now, what did it matter? She was a married woman and while it might cause some scandal, it couldn't be any worse than what either of them had already faced. Besides, the few servants he employed were loyal, especially to Prudence, he had noticed.

In the meantime, he hadn't returned to Angelo's, and he hadn't arranged any further fencing matches.

He did, however, invite Prudence to join him one day when she returned.

Benedict couldn't have said what had come over him. But he had been practicing – alone, of course – and had just left his fencing room when he had seen her enter the house, similarly dressed. And while he knew that her fencing against another man and going to Angelo's had been, essentially, part of their agreement, he was taken aback by the heady sensation of jealousy that had overcome him when he considered it.

He didn't know if it was the thought of her surrounded by other men, of her practicing her skills with another opponent, or trusting damn Hugo Conway to protect her, but he had an overwhelming urge to be the one to fulfill all those roles for her.

Which had led to him, before he could even think about what he was doing, asking her if she would like to practice with him.

She had looked at him in surprise but then nodded her agreement.

It had been his most invigorating match to date.

He was a smart enough man to separate fencing and sexual relations in his mind, but now, after what had happened the last time they had faced off against one another in this room, he wasn't sure that he could ever completely disconnect the two – not when Prudence was involved.

By the time they had finished, they were sweating, panting, and both aroused.

This time, at least, they had made it to the bedroom.

And so they continued – tied together physically, but never speaking of anything that mattered. He still ate dinner alone in his study, didn't join her for breakfast, and subtly encouraged her to leave nearly immediately after their time together at night.

He could sense her want for something more, but he certainly couldn't give her that something. He had told her exactly that before this had all started, so it was fair, wasn't it?

Except now, the more time he spent with her, the more he realized that perhaps it wasn't just Prudence who longed for something more.

Perhaps it was Benedict himself.

* * *

PRUDENCE BRACED herself as she knocked on Juliana's door.

Her sister's home was nothing at all like the mansion where they had been raised. In fact, Juliana's small townhouse could likely fit into the drawing room of Warwick House.

But it was filled entirely with love – and also many, many animals.

A bit of jealousy surfaced. Not over the animals, but at the connection Juliana and her husband, Matthew, shared. He might be a detective and lacking the status, connection, and wealth of any other man who Juliana could have married, but he loved her and treated her better than any other person ever could.

For which Prudence was grateful. Her sister deserved to be looked after.

Matthew also didn't have any problem with Juliana collecting strays, and had presented her with Lucy, the little street mongrel Juliana had fallen in love with, as a wedding gift. But Lucy had come with Max, a much larger, shaggier, more exuberant former stray. Soon the cats followed, and Prudence actually wasn't entirely sure just how Juliana had ended up with the bird. Prudence wasn't certain if her sister had added anyone else to her collection since the last time she had visited.

"Pru!" Juliana opened the door a crack, likely to prevent anyone from attempting to escape. "Come in, come in. Just be careful, for we have a new member in our household and he keeps trying to get out."

"Is he friendly?"

"Of course," Juliana said, and as Prudence slipped through the door, a huge dog that looked more like a small pony came barrelling toward them.

"Juliana!" Prudence exclaimed, holding her hands out in front of her as the dog skidded to a stop in front of her. "This isn't a dog. This is a horse!"

Juliana laughed, even though Prudence hadn't been jesting.

"He is a dog, not to worry. He was supposed to be a hunter, but he doesn't seem to possess any ability to track a scent, and so his owner got rid of him. Just sent him away. Can you imagine?"

While Prudence would never love animals with the same

dedication as Juliana, she couldn't imagine doing so to a creature, either.

"No, of course not," she said. "But are you sure you have room for him? Wouldn't he be better in a country home or at least a larger townhouse?"

The dog produced a tongue that was as large as Prudence's hand, a fact which she gathered when it filled the entirety of it upon his lick.

"Pru!" Juliana said, her eyes lighting up. "Are you saying you want him?"

"Oh, goodness, no," Prudence said, imagining what Benedict would say if she brought home such a dog. "I mean..." He was staring at her now with his tongue lolling out of his mouth, his hazel eyes with their flecks of gold wide and supplicating.

He certainly was awfully friendly, and when he sat in front of her like this, practically begging for her to pet him, she had to consider that maybe it would help ease some of her loneliness. Benedict might have opened his body to her, but he still barely grunted a few words at a time to her. She only saw him when they fenced or made love – if one could call it that.

"You like him," Juliana said, beaming at her.

"I—" She did. She really *did* like this dog. "I can try, but I cannot make any promises to keep him. Perhaps in time."

"Oh, wonderful," Juliana said, clapping her hands together as she beamed at her sister, and Prudence looked at her with suspicion.

"This isn't why you invited me here, was it?"

"No, of course not," Juliana said, shaking her head, as she led her the few steps toward their small sitting area, the dogs following them. "I hadn't seen you in so long. I want to know how... well, *everything*, is going."

"Life is... interesting."

Juliana tilted her head. "Is your husband kind to you?"

Ah, so they had already arrived at the heart of the matter. Juliana was concerned for her wellbeing. Prudence did appreciate that, for she would fear the same for Juliana had she married a man who they barely knew, was suspected of murder, and rumored to be a recluse.

"I know you can take care of yourself," Juliana continued. "But—"

"But we feared that Benedict had killed our father and threatened our family," Prudence completed for her. "I know. And as far as I am aware, he had nothing to do with Father's death. I haven't been able to find anything that would suggest it."

"How hard have you searched?"

Prudence bit her lip. The truth was, she *hadn't* been searching overly hard. She had been too afraid that if Benedict caught her, any steps they had taken forward together would all come crashing down.

"I search when I can," she said evasively. "It is difficult, for Benedict is most often in his study, where I'm sure he would hide anything incriminating."

"I see," Juliana said suspiciously. "Have you heard any more about the vowels he holds?"

Prudence shook her head. "He tells me it is all business, which I understand. However, I have seen the ledger book, and he holds a great many vowels which belong to a great many men. I also overheard a man one day ask him for more time to pay them back, and Benedict refused. He has a heartless side, that is for certain."

"But not with you?"

Prudence hesitated. How did she explain it?

"He has made... parts of himself vulnerable." The physical

parts. "I think there is more to it. That he is hiding who he truly is and what has made him keep himself so guarded. But I cannot get him to open up. If he did, then maybe there could be more to our marriage. But until then..." She shrugged half-heartedly, hating the pitying stare that Juliana was throwing her way.

"As long as you are safe."

"I am. Of course, I am." She leaned forward, regarding Juliana with intensity. "If I ever felt that I was in danger, I would leave. I promise you that."

Juliana smiled without humour. "We are all in danger at all times, though, are we not?"

Prudence sighed. "Apparently. Did Matthew say anything about how the chandelier fell?"

Juliana nodded. "He did say that it had been cut so that it would be likely to fall. He found a small stone close by, so he believes that someone must have arranged for something to be thrown at it from a nearby balcony."

Prudence shivered despite herself. "Has he discovered anything else or determined if there are any other suspects?"

Juliana shrugged herself now. "He hasn't been particularly eager to share anything with me lately. I think he is concerned that it might influence my behaviour toward anyone he is investigating. But he said that he is getting closer, that there are those who had vengeances against Father that are too great to ignore."

"Interesting," Prudence murmured. "Has he said anything about Benedict?"

"No," Juliana said, shaking her head. "Nothing to me, at least."

"Will you share with me if he does?"

"Of course."

For even though her suspicion of Benedict was what had brought her to him, the truth was, Prudence couldn't help but hope that it would soon be proven he had absolutely nothing to do with the threat that hung over them all.

For if she knew with all certainty that he was innocent, that would be the start of something more.

She was sure of it.

CHAPTER 17

"*We* are having company tonight. Be sure you are available for dinner."

"Pardon me?" Prudence's head snapped up in surprise. "Did you say company? You do not have company."

"Usually not. But for these people I must make an exception."

"These people?" Prudence felt like a parrot, but she wasn't sure how else she was going to encourage him to share with her what was happening.

"My aunt. My brother and his wife."

"Your family, then."

"Yes. Oh, and my brother's children."

"I see," Prudence murmured. She hadn't met the children before, and she hadn't had a proper conversation with the rest of his family since, well, the night they had caught Benedict with his hand down her bodice as he attempted to recover the page she had stolen from his ledger.

"You will be at dinner?"

Prudence looked up once more from the writing table in front of her where she sat in the corner of the parlor. She had been painstakingly writing in the script belonging to Peter Robertson, one that she hoped appeared darker and more masculine than her own, responding to mail from potential opponents and fans who followed him.

She narrowed her eyes at Benedict now, wondering why he would even ask such a thing.

"I am at dinner every night," she said succinctly. "It is you who will have to appear where you are usually absent."

He opened his mouth as if he were about to respond to that but, obviously considering that, perhaps, she might be right, instead he turned on his heel and walked away.

Leaving Prudence to grin in satisfaction that she had produced a barb to which he was unable to respond with a proper comeback.

A smile which remained until later in the day when her nerves began to set on edge at the thought of facing his family once more.

She never had the opportunity to explain to them what she had been doing in Benedict's study that night. And, even if she had, what was she supposed to say? That she had broken into his house in an attempt to investigate him, to determine if he had killed her father? That surely wouldn't endear her to them.

No, best to allow them to continue to think that she was a harlot who had been either attempting to seduce Benedict or was meeting with him in a mutual yet forbidden liaison. At least that had a romantic air about it, did it not?

"They are not that bad," Benedict murmured as they waited in the drawing room for his family to arrive, and she realized that she had been fidgeting with her gown.

"I never made any suggestion *they* were," she said, raising an eyebrow as she made it clear just who she was referring to.

He snorted but didn't respond, for at that moment the door opened, and Jefferson announced their guests.

"My lord, my lady, Lady Emily and Mr. and Mrs. Gallagher have arrived."

Prudence lifted the smile she had perfected over her lifetime to her face and prepared to greet them but was completely taken aback when three children raced past the disapproving Jefferson and into the room.

"Uncle Benedict!" they cried, two of them throwing themselves into Benedict's arms. Prudence waited for him to brush them off, to tell them that this was unseemly, that they had no business in even being in the drawing room, let alone jumping into his arms – but then he smiled.

A true smile. One that stretched across his face and reflected in his eyes, that was not a façade or one that only appeared when he was grimly satisfied with an achievement or a point in a fencing match, but one that appeared to come straight from his heart.

"Oliver, Alexander, it is good to see you. It has been too long," he said, ruffling their hair as he set them on their feet before turning to the smallest child, the little girl who was standing there shyly watching her brothers. "Liliana, you are so patient. Come here," he said, holding out his arms and she stepped into his embrace before wrapping her slender arms around him, obviously adoring him as much as her brothers did.

It was then that Prudence's heart not only softened but melted right at his feet.

For here was the man that she had guessed existed deep within him, underneath all the layers of rigid armor he had clad around himself. Here was the heart she had been searching for, the one he pretended didn't exist. Here was the man who could be a father if he ever so chose.

And here was a man who could love and accept love in

return, if he would but allow it.

"He is more than what most people think," a voice murmured in her ear, and Prudence turned to find Lady Emily standing next to her. Lady Emily was an acquaintance of Prudence's mother, and while she didn't know her overly well, she had always seemed a reasonable woman.

"Is he always like this with the children?" Prudence asked softly so that no one else would hear her question.

"He is," she confirmed. "They just adore him. They see a side of him that not many others do."

Prudence watched Benedict to ensure that he wasn't aware they were speaking of him.

"But why is he not..."

"Like this all the time?" Lady Emily finished for her with a chuckle. "I believe he feels he has nothing to prove with the children. That they do not judge him, and he is able to be himself with them."

"I see," Prudence murmured, unable to tear her eyes away from him.

"If nothing else, he will be a wonderful father one day," Lady Emily said, causing Prudence to blink back a few tears for what Benedict had told her would never happen. "I know you've likely had your doubts, but Benedict... he's had some challenges in his life. Ones that have made him into the man he is today, have caused him to guard himself very closely."

Prudence could do no more than nod as she hoped, deep within her, that one day he would trust her enough to share the truth of who he was and what had happened to him.

* * *

BENEDICT COULD FEEL Prudence watching him that night after his family left. She stood at the bottom of the staircase, her eyes on his back as he began to walk toward his study. There were a few things he wanted to take care of before retiring for the night.

"Is something amiss?" he asked with some annoyance, mostly at himself for stopping to speak to her and caring enough about what she was thinking to voice the question.

"Your niece and nephews love you," she said, some bewilderment in her tone, which he supposed was understandable for he was not exactly a man who would appear to be fond of children.

"They are good children," was all he said, turning to leave, but then he heard a step behind him.

"Benedict?" she said, her voice serious and he stilled as silence around them filled with tension.

"Yes?"

"What happened?"

He knew she wasn't talking about this evening or even the most recent future. She was asking him what had made him into the man he was today. She was no fool. He was sure she understood that he hadn't always been like this, that there was a reason he kept himself hidden from the rest of the world.

His first inclination was to tell her that his past was none of her concern and she should continue on as they had from the start. But how could he when she had, if nothing else, shared her secret, her body, her life with him, had put up with his surliness to this point, had been willing to share all of herself with him?

He knew that what they had together was never going to last, but he supposed he owed her part of the truth, after she had not only done as he asked and been the dutiful wife at dinner, but had entertained his family, acting the perfect hostess even when he knew she likely wasn't completely comfortable with hosting them after their beginnings. She had never pried, had never pushed, had never asked anything of him – until now.

"I lost my parents when I was young."

"Yes, for which I am sorry. I can hardly imagine it."

"My father… he was destroyed by a man who took everything from him. My father was not particularly adept at managing accounts and estates, unfortunately. When he was at his lowest, when he had lost nearly all that he had available to him, this… man told him of an investment opportunity. One that he assured him would make him back all that he needed to restore his fortunes. Trusting him, for they were friends at the time and the man had a high reputation, my father agreed and gave him all that he had remaining."

Prudence stared at him from across the room, her lips parted, and he wondered if she had even an inkling of who it was that had done his father so much wrong.

"And then he lost everything?" she asked when Benedict didn't continue, finding that he needed a moment to compose himself to ensure that he didn't show her any of the emotion that was washing over him as though it was happening all over again.

"He didn't lose it," he said, hearing the censure in his voice, even though it was, of course, not her fault at all. "It was stolen from him. There was never an investment opportunity. It was all a scheme to steal from others."

"Your father wasn't able to get it back? Or go to anyone who could help?"

"What was he to do?" Benedict asked bitterly. "To admit that he had been so taken in would be utter embarrassment. He was already so ashamed. He had not only been played for a fool, but he had nothing left, no way to support his family, nor all the people who relied on him. So he…"

He ran a hand through his hair, turning away from her so that she couldn't see his face as he breathed in, realizing that he had never actually shared this story before. His brother had an inkling of the truth, but Benedict had never even told *him* every detail, preferring that Martin believe their father had no faults, that he was a man he could always look up to and hold in high regard – for it was not as though Benedict could ever be the best role model for Martin or Martin's children.

"He took his own life," he admitted, the words tumbling out before he could rein them in. He waited for Prudence to chastise his father for such a cowardly act, as he was sure most people would see it. They had been careful to cover it up, so that his father would receive a proper burial and the family would not be shunned, but Benedict would never be able to forget the image of his father hanging in his study when he went to call him in for dinner.

Warm hands slid across his upper arms, and before he could stop her, Prudence's body was pressed against his back, her cheek against his shoulder as she embraced him from behind.

"Oh, Benedict," she said, and he listened for pity but instead heard sadness in her tone. "How awful. I am so sorry."

If only she knew that she was apologizing for her own father's actions. But that, he could not share.

"I found him," he said, his voice hoarse. "And then a month later, I found my mother. She took ill immediately after my father passed. She was never particularly strong to begin with. We will never know for certain what she died of, but Aunt Emily, who raised us until we were old enough to be on our own, always said that it was a broken heart."

Prudence nodded into his back, her arms squeezing tighter around him.

"I can understand why you would not want to love again, to allow anyone, especially children, into your heart," she said. "The fear of loving and losing can be difficult to overcome. But Benedict… those children, Martin's children, they love you. And you love them. Sometimes people enter your heart whether you welcome them or not."

Benedict ran a hand over his face, disappointed in himself that what she said was true. For someday, his niece and nephews would discover what kind of man he truly was, and they would hate him for it.

"It is not just that," he said, even though she had touched on an inkling of the truth. "They may love me, but I am not worthy of that love. I am not a good man, Prudence, and you must realize that as well."

"Everyone is worthy of love," she said fiercely, as he remembered her saying so before. She walked around him so that she was facing him, reaching up to cup her hands around his cheeks as her green eyes bore into his imploringly. "I know that you keep me at a distance because you do not want us growing close to one another. But Benedict, I believe we would be better facing all that is against us together instead of alone, do you not?"

Perhaps they would be – until she realized that it was her own family who had ruined his, that he wouldn't rest until they felt the same pain that he had.

"I am sorry that I cannot give you more," he said gruffly, and he saw the hurt on her face at what he was sure she considered a denial. "You are a better woman than most, Prudence. I do not deserve you."

"You could if you tried," she said softly, and Benedict had never hated himself more than he did in that moment, knowing he had disappointed her.

"I shall do my best," he relented, and when she stepped

toward him and embraced him once more, he felt worse than he ever had before, for now he was lying to her.

He would never be able to fully let her in. Not when she had Remington blood running through her veins.

He could but wish that it was otherwise.

CHAPTER 18

*P*rudence tied her bonnet under her chin and nodded to Jefferson before stepping out the door into the sunshine the next morning. She felt somewhat lighter now that Benedict had opened up to her, even though she felt that there was more he wasn't sharing.

But they had taken a step forward together, and that was more than she would ever have thought possible a very short time ago.

"Prudence?"

She turned to find him purposefully striding toward her through the open door.

"What's wrong?" she asked.

"Where are you going?" he asked, and while his voice was as gruff as ever, it was not quite as demanding as it would have been previously.

"To Warwick House," she said. "I received a note that my family wants to meet."

"Can I see it?"

"The note?"

"Yes," he said, holding out his hand, and she frowned but,

not seeing any issue in sharing it, found it in her reticule and passed it to him.

"Is this your sister's script?"

"Yes, of course," she said, furrowing her brow. "Why?"

"You are leaving the house alone, dressed as yourself, responding to a note that could have come from anyone. You have to be sure that this is not someone trying to take advantage of you."

Prudence could feel the incredulity growing on her face.

"Why, Benedict, are you taking care to look after me?" she asked, her heart warming at the thought.

"I promised your brother I would," he grumbled.

She couldn't suppress a smile at his inability to admit that he was concerned for her. "I am perfectly fine walking alone," she said. "It is the middle of the day, and it is but a short stroll through Mayfair. Besides, I have a weapon," she said, patting her thigh where her dagger was tied into her skirts.

"If you were anyone else, that would only further concern me," he said with a sigh. "But I have time. I shall walk you there."

"It really is not necessary," she said, shaking her head, knowing that he likely wouldn't appreciate having to take the time out of his day, but he was already urging her toward the street. "I insist."

Prudence couldn't help but steal glances at him as they walked along, his cane tapping with each step. He seemed different today, and she wondered if opening up to her had caused him to feel more inclined to treat her as his wife in more than name. Every day she was becoming further convinced that they could have a future together if they could just learn to trust one another and overcome the beginning of their marriage.

As they walked toward Warwick House, Prudence risked looking over her shoulder. It was not as though she wasn't accustomed to being more apprehensive than before her father's death, but today she had this strange feeling that she was being followed.

"Do you feel that?" she asked Benedict, who looked down at her with question. "That someone is watching us?"

"Perhaps everyone is watching us. We caused quite a scandal when we married and are rarely seen together."

"Perhaps," she murmured, but she didn't think that was it. A tickle was beginning at her neck, an unwelcome one that was threatening to creep down her spine. "Thank you for walking me."

"Of course," he said as Warwick House came into view.

Prudence cast her gaze over her shoulder once more but didn't see anyone paying any bit of attention to them. "You are welcome to come in with me," she said as his steps began to slow in front of the gate. "This is a family meeting, and you are, after all, my husband. You have joined us before."

He stared up at the house, casting his eyes over it with distaste.

"It is rather ostentatious, isn't it?" she said, looking up at it, trying to see it through the eyes of someone who did not grow up within its walls. "Giles and Emma hardly know what to do with it. Giles was not here often, as we spent so much of our childhoods in the country, away from Father."

When Benedict looked at her then, there was a hardness in his gaze that took her slightly off guard, and she wondered if she had said something wrong. Perhaps he was simply wishing that he'd had his own parents through his childhood.

"Our father was not exactly a good man," she said softly. "I am sure you have heard the tales about him."

He nodded slowly, his expression giving away nothing until he finally spoke.

"I appreciate the invitation to accompany you," he said, the guard in his voice returned, "but I have business to take care of elsewhere in Mayfair. I will return in an hour to walk you home."

"Very well," she said, even though it was slightly disappointing that he didn't want to take the opportunity to come in to greet her family, especially as she had spent an enjoyable evening with his just the night before.

One genuine conversation and here she had considered the two of them were in a true relationship.

He nodded and stepped back, obviously waiting for her to enter. She pushed open the gate and ascended the stairs, trying to smile at him as she waved her farewell while Jameson opened the door to her. Benedict cared – she knew that. Otherwise, he would never have invited her into his bed, would not be taking steps to ensure her safety.

He was *choosing* to keep himself from her. How was she ever going to convince him that he deserved more than what he was allowing himself?

She had to shrug the thought away, however, as she entered Warwick house, nearly shocked for a moment at the light, warmth, and laughter that washed over her. She beamed as she heard fingernails against the floor, and soon enough a familiar dog rushed out of the drawing room toward her.

"Prudence, there you are," Juliana said, following him out. "We were becoming worried about you."

"I had an escort," she said. "Benedict walked me here. You brought Angus."

"Did you ask Benedict about him?"

"No," Prudence said, biting her lip. "I completely forgot."

There was far too much else that had been on her mind.

"Next time?" she asked with a forced smile, and Juliana looked at her with some uncertainty, but shrugged her shoulders as they returned to the room. Everyone had gathered, even their mother sitting on the edge of one of the delicate pink and white chairs, eyeing Angus with distaste.

"That mongrel belongs in the stables, Juliana," she said, staring down her nose at him, and Prudence couldn't help but take offence, even though the dog had been in her care for all of two minutes.

"He seems quite clean," she attempted, which caused her mother's stare to turn upon her now.

"He is the size of a horse."

"A pony, perhaps," Prudence countered, and Lady Winchester snorted as she stared the dog up and down.

"Does he do his business outside?" she asked, to which Juliana nodded.

"Very well. He can stay."

Prudence's mother stared at her own mother. "Since when are you in charge here?"

"Since the day I joined you in this house," Lady Winchester said with a sniff. "You just never quite realized it."

Prudence had to turn her laugh into a cough when her mother stared at her in irritation at her grandmother's words, but she couldn't help herself. Her grandmother had a way of always getting to the truth before anyone else ever did.

"Tea, Prudence?" her mother asked with pursed lips, ignoring Lady Winchester, and Prudence nodded and accepted before Giles strode to the middle of the room.

"Thank you all for coming," he said, before Juliana sighed, interrupting him.

"These meetings are becoming all too familiar," she said, to which Giles nodded, his shoulders tight, and Prudence realized that she missed the lighthearted man her brother had been before all this.

"I agree. And I am hopeful that soon enough we will be done with it."

"You have been saying that for months," Prudence interjected. "I think everyone is about ready to come to the conclusion of this mystery."

"We have all been ready for some time, Pru," Giles said, "but we haven't wanted to take any risks. As it is…" He hesitated for a second, a pained expression crossing his face, before he looked toward Juliana and Matthew. "Why do I not let Archibald explain what he has discovered?"

Matthew nodded and stood, hands in his pockets.

"We've had a couple of facts to come to light, and I believe we are close to discovering who is behind the threats to the family and your father's murder. We have had our suspicions for a time, however… there will be repercussions, no matter who is at fault."

"I do not like the sound of this," their mother said, and Matthew nodded to her but continued speaking.

"We accused someone too hastily before," Matthew said, with a glance over at Hudson, their half-brother, who Giles had prematurely blamed based on false evidence. "I would advise that we do not do so again."

"Matthew, we appreciate your discretion, but we are on edge waiting for you to tell us what you have found," Emma said politely, although Prudence could see the flash of impatience in her eyes.

"Very well," Matthew said before he looked over at Prudence, and fear leaped in her heart when she saw the concern in his eyes – concern that was directed at her. "The first information we have discovered is regarding Lord Trundelle."

Prudence blinked rapidly, wishing she had heard incorrectly, though knew that it was not the case.

"What about him?" she asked, surprised at the steadiness

of her voice.

"When he was a boy, his father took his own life," Matthew said, causing Prudence's mother to gasp in outraged shock.

"We were told he had an apoplexy!"

"No," Matthew shook his head. "He lost everything, and he was obviously too ashamed to continue living."

Prudence looked down at the floor, feeling all eyes on her. She was surprised to find that anger was simmering in her belly at her entire family sitting here and speaking of Benedict's past as though it somehow made him guilty, when in fact, it had been a tragedy that had befallen him at far too young of an age.

"I fail to see what this has to do with the threat to our family," she said, an edge in her voice as she met Matthew's eyes now, annoyed by the pity she saw within them.

"The previous Lord Trundelle found himself in a bad situation. That cannot be blamed on anyone else. But then, the last of his fortune was basically stolen by none other than the Duke of Warwick."

Now *that* was news to Prudence, and her mouth dropping open in surprise. Her father had been the one who convinced Lord Trundelle to invest all his money in an illicit scheme? Why would Benedict not have mentioned that? Unless... unless he blamed her father and her family for everything he had gone through. Not only for his father's death, but his mother's as well. For breaking apart his entire family.

Matthew took a breath and then went on. "I believe that the current Lord Trundelle placed the fault on your father for everything he had lost. Since that time, he has built up the family's fortunes once more, most of it through buying up vowels of other noblemen and then cashing them in. I believe Giles can speak more to this."

"I feel a fool for not knowing this sooner," he said, "but he has focused on the men who were Father's acquaintances. I believe he is trying to ruin them all as his family was ruined. Our family must not only be on his list but likely his ultimate goal."

"How could he possibly ruin our family?" Prudence asked, trying to ignore how her body seemed to have turned wooden, her jaw tensing as she stared at her brother. "We do not owe him anything – do we?"

Even as she asked, she remembered the page from the ledger book, the one she had not been able to completely peruse, which had Giles' name written on the top.

Except perhaps it hadn't been Giles' name. Perhaps it was their father's.

"I believe we might," Giles said. "I need to speak to my man-of-business once more, but there must be something that Lord Trundelle has over us. Something big. It has me… concerned."

Giles was never overly concerned. This couldn't be good.

"There's something else," Matthew continued, and Prudence turned a wary gaze upon him. How could there be anything worse than this?

"Lord Trundelle – the current one – was to be married a few years ago. Apologies, Prudence, if this comes as a surprise or causes you any alarm. It was not official, so it didn't cause a scandal when the marriage did not go ahead. However, it was all but announced. Then the Duke of Warwick became involved. He knew the young lady's father, told both him and the woman that Trundelle was liable to hurt her. Because Trundelle was already such a recluse, the family ended up declining the marriage."

"And then I went and married my own sister off to him," Giles said with a snort, turning from them and running a hand through his hair. "What does that make me?"

"You were doing what you thought was best," Prudence

said, standing and placing her hand on his arm before turning to the rest of the room with her hands on her hips.

"I did not know the full story to this, I will admit that," she said. "But are we forgetting that Benedict was not even here when Father died or when Juliana's abduction occurred? How could he have anything to do with this? Is it not a stretch to blame Father's death on him simply because he had reason to hate him? So did many other people."

"This is true, although he always could have paid someone to do the work for him," Matthew said. "I should note, however, that we do have another suspect. First, I wanted you to know the possibility of Trundelle's involvement, so that, if nothing else, you can be careful."

"Prudence, I think it would be best that you leave Trundelle's house and stay here with us," Giles said, crossing his arms over his chest. "Then we will know you are safe."

Prudence turned to him. "You want me to leave my husband and what has become my home? Just what would I say to him? 'I am sorry, Benedict, but my family believes that you are, after all, the one who murdered my father and is trying to kill my brother'? Besides, none of this is rational. If he ever had any inkling to hurt me, he has had plenty of opportunity! But he has done nothing."

"He is kind to you, then?" Maria asked softly, and Prudence nodded.

"I would not say that he is the most affectionate man in the world, but he is good to me, yes."

Giles sighed and ran a hand through his hair. "I cannot force you to do anything you do not want to do, Prudence. You are married now, and I am no longer the one who is supposed to look after you. But if anything happened, I would forever blame myself. I was the one who convinced you that you were better off married to him than embroiled in a scandal."

"I have no one to blame but myself," Prudence said. "It was I who broke into his house and found myself in a compromising position with him."

"You were only there because you suspected him," Giles pointed out, and she nodded.

"True. And if anyone had the opportunity to discover any reason he might be guilty, it would be me. But I have not. He is a different man because of what our father did to him, and his past explains a lot regarding his current outlook on life. But I do not believe that we should blame him for all our problems because of it. He is a victim as much as the rest of us."

And as she defended her husband, Prudence realized one thing: she was not saying this because she was a dutiful wife. She always believed in discovering the truth, which had led her to where she was today.

No, she was defending Benedict because she believed in him. Because she had feelings for him. Because… because she loved him.

She sat there rigidly as the realization washed over her, causing both a heady sensation to fill her as well as a slight bit of panic.

She didn't know how it was possible that she could feel so strongly for him – not after his surliness nor his grouchiness nor the way he kept her at arm's length from him.

But he had also provided her glimpses of who he truly was, of how he cared about her and his family, even as he tried so hard not to.

Now she just had to convince him of how she felt, to tell him the truth. She believed in him, no matter what others said about him.

And that he could trust her with the entire truth – no matter how terrible it might be.

CHAPTER 19

*B*enedict sat outside Warwick House, watching for the front doors to open and for Prudence to emerge.

He had no idea how he had turned into such a lovesick fool that he would sit outside a house and wait for a woman, but here he was. He had tried to walk around Mayfair, but the truth was, he had no other business to take care of. He was only here because of Prudence but he had no interest in sitting down with the rest of the Remingtons.

He had watched her as she had prepared to depart that afternoon. She had been leaving, as she usually did, alone, even though he knew that Conway often met her to walk with her.

Yet there was something that struck at his heart that she never relied on him, that while he might be her husband, he was not the first person she would ever ask to accompany her or to look out for her.

And, in that moment, he had realized that, against every better judgement he had, he wanted to be.

Besides, while he knew she could protect herself better

than most women, the thought of her coming to any harm was now more than he could bear.

He didn't want to consider what that meant.

What was taking so long? He tapped his cane on the ground impatiently, surprised when a shadow fell over his feet.

"Lord Trundelle. I would not have expected to find you here."

"Hemingway," he grunted, having no particular interest in making pleasantries with Prudence's cousin. He still hadn't forgiven the man for leaving her moments before the chandelier fell upon her. He had meant to ask Archibald what had become of his interrogation of him after that, but it was not as though he and Archibald were bosom buddies. "My wife is within."

"You did not accompany her, then? I suppose I can see why you wouldn't. They are a rather intimidating lot, are they not? And that house... is something else entirely."

"I imagine you have spent a great deal of time within it."

"Of course, of course," Hemingway said, bobbing his head, and Benedict recalled from his few interactions with the man that he was one of the types who always said what he thought those around him wanted to hear. "My mother and the dowager duchess have always been quite close."

"As have you and the current duke?"

Hemingway tilted his head to the side. "He was gone for a great deal of my life, but we have become close once again, yes."

"Are you joining the family today?" Benedict asked, and Hemingway nodded once more.

"My mother is visiting. She took the carriage while I agreed to meet her here, for I had a previous engagement. Ah, here she is now."

A black lacquer carriage pulled up in front of the house,

the footman and driver quickly opening the door and pulling out the stairs once the horses and carriage came to a stop. Hemingway rose and held out a hand for a woman who must be Lady Hemingway. As she descended, she looked down her nose at Benedict as though he was a cockroach who was not supposed to be there.

"Lord Trundelle," she said, disapproval in her tone. "Why are you loitering outside like a commoner?"

Benedict started at that, even as he stood to greet her.

"I had other business to attend to, Lady Hemingway," he said tersely. "Now I am waiting for my wife."

Lady Hemingway sniffed. "I see." She took a step toward Benedict, and there was something in her eye that he immediately recognized, that he didn't overly appreciate – disapproval. "I knew your father," she said, which caused Benedict's spine to straighten.

"Did you now?" he said, to which she nodded as the corners of her mouth began to spread slightly.

"He had his troubles, of course, but he was always quite kind to me. They were good friends, your father, my husband, and the Duke of Warwick."

Benedict kept his lips tightly shut, for he had no wish to speak of his father with this woman – not if she was associating him with the duke. He tilted his head to the side as he stared at her. Did she have any idea of what had actually happened, of the scheme the duke had pulled? Or was she trying to bait him?

"How interesting that our families have joined one another once again," she said, to which Benedict slowly nodded.

"Your husband was a cousin of the duke's, was he not?" he asked her.

"Yes. Why?"

"Only because it is not as though you are actually part of the Remington family, now, are you?"

She narrowed her eyes and took a step toward him, allowing Benedict the opportunity to see that he had struck a chord within her.

"I will have you know—"

"Mother," Hemingway interjected as he stepped in front of her, taking her arm and turning her around. "I believe we should get to your visit."

Had the two of them been invited to this family meeting?

Hemingway turned around with a friendly smile toward Benedict. "Good day, Lord Trundelle. We hope to see you again soon."

The door opened just as they stepped in front of it, and Benedict watched them stop to speak to someone who was emerging from within the entrance. Once they moved out of the way, he was able to see that it was Prudence.

He hated that the smile grew on his face just at seeing her, that his heart swelled and he was filled with a bloody brightness that he had tried to rid himself of for years now.

It was, however, just like when he saw his niece and nephew – an indescribable happiness that he didn't wish for, that he had been trying to avoid.

But here it was.

She called to him – her independence, her strength, her heart, her ability to see past the barriers he had erected around himself for the man who was underneath. She had never given up on him, no matter how surly he had been, but instead continued to fight for him and for them.

He loved her.

Bloody hell.

And there was nothing he could do about it.

He couldn't tell her. He couldn't ask for more. He couldn't do anything that would deepen the bond between them, for it would only hurt both of them more when it came time to sever it. All he could do was ensure that when he hurt her – he didn't want to, but he knew he would – it was with as much compassion and kindness as was possible.

Even as he considered it, he looked up to find her walking down the stairs toward him, the smile stretching over her face in greeting. As she neared, however, he could see trouble hidden within her green eyes, putting him instantly on alert.

"Is everything all right?" he asked, and she nodded.

"Yes, I believe so. There are a few things we should discuss, but it can wait until we arrive home."

Home. The word coming off her tongue, describing the house the two of them shared, meant more to him than he could properly explain, even to himself.

But it was true. It was a building they shared together, where they had begun to build a life together, whether he had asked for it or not.

"Hemingway was not invited to the meeting, then?" he asked as they turned toward Portman Square.

"No," she said, shaking her head. "I did not even know he was arriving. His mother was calling upon mine, although I'm not sure that she was aware to expect them. It is interesting timing…"

"Why is that?"

"It is just something that Matthew said. When he was… well, when he was telling us of whom he suspected, he mentioned Lord Hemingway."

"He also has his suspicions, then?" Benedict asked with tight lips.

"He said there are a few clues pointing in Lord Hemingway's direction," she said. "I believe he has suspected him for some time but knew that Giles would not be pleased about it – and, as it turns out, he was right. But there is the fact that Lord Hemingway left me when the chandelier fell, of course.

And now Matthew is wondering if his alibi for Juliana's abduction is as accurate as he originally thought. Of course, he does have motive – perhaps as much motive as anyone does, although Father had a great many enemies. But at this point, if anything happened to Giles, Lord Hemingway would become the next duke, for Giles and Emma's first baby is a girl."

"Of course," Benedict muttered, as the truth was becoming rather clear. "Promise me something, Prudence."

"What is it?"

"You are a stubborn woman," he muttered at the fact she couldn't agree without first knowing what she was promising. "Do not go near Hemingway. Do not investigate him on your own. Do not leave the house without me."

"Without you?" she asked, leaning back and blinking up at him. "Then I will never go anywhere!"

"I will take you where you want to go. Just ask."

"What if Hugo accompanies me?"

"No," Benedict shook his head. "He will not have the same urgency to protect you."

Benedict kept his eyes forward, but he could feel her gaze upon him.

"Why not?"

"Because—" Because Hugo Conway did not love her as Benedict did. "Because he is not your husband," he finished lamely.

"Very well," Prudence surprisingly relented with a sigh. "Let us hope that this all comes to a conclusion relatively quickly."

He nodded as his – their – townhouse came into view, and he held his hand out as they walked up the steps, greeting Jefferson when they arrived. Prudence hesitated in the foyer, and Benedict looked up at her expectantly.

"Was there something else you wished to discuss?"

"Yes," she said with a nod. "Could we go upstairs?"

"It is the middle of the day."

"I wish to be alone for this conversation."

"Very well," he said warily, for he could see the hesitation on her face, as though this was a conversation she was not particularly looking forward to, which made him wonder just how he would be feeling about it.

He followed her into her bedchamber, noting that she had made a few changes in the canopy, the curtains, and the bedding, but before he could comment, she turned around and pushed him down so that he was sitting on the edge of her bed.

"Before I ask you what I need to ask you, there is something I need to tell you."

"Very well," he said, holding his breath at what she could possibly have learned about him.

"I love you."

Benedict sat there in shocked silence, blinking up at her as she stared down at him, her eyes glistening with unshed tears.

It was everything he should ever want to hear. That a woman he loved more than she could possibly imagine felt such a way for him in return. That they could start building a life together. That, no matter what she had just learned about him, she still was able to love him, especially after he had been so terrible toward her.

He knew what she wanted to hear. But he also remembered what he had promised himself – that he would be sure to minimize her pain as much as possible.

"You do not."

She blinked at him, her expression hardening.

"Do not tell me how I feel," she said, placing her hands on her hips in a gesture that was so Prudence he would have laughed had it been any other situation. "I am not asking you.

I am telling you. No matter how hard you have tried to prevent me from doing so, I love you. And after everything we went through, I am glad we married, and further than that, even if you never meant to, you have shown me the true side of yourself, a man who is not only worthy of love, but also capable of it himself, if you would just allow yourself."

He stared up at her incredulously. She was far too good for him, that was for certain. What had he ever done to deserve her? And why had he been given such a gift in her, if it was all for not?

He stood, cupping her face in his hands urgently, needing her to understand.

"You shouldn't," he whispered, and she tilted her head up to his.

"But I do," she said, the moment before their lips met.

He would never be able to tell her how he felt for her. But in this moment, before all would eventually come crashing down upon them, he could, at the very least, show her.

CHAPTER 20

*P*rudence knew that he might never tell her what she wanted to hear, but she *felt* his returned emotion, deep within her. She was a practical woman, and had another woman told her of this, she likely would have told her that she was nothing but a lovesick fool.

She couldn't have said how she knew, but she did. Benedict loved her in return.

He was too afraid to admit it, but the way he was currently making love to her mouth said enough.

She groaned into him, and suddenly she needed more. She needed to show him what he did to her, and perhaps, it would allow him to truly understand.

She ran her hands down his chest, lifting them underneath his jacket and waistcoat until she was able to tug his shirt out of his breeches, giving her space to slip one hand underneath until she found his shaft, keeping her grip loose as she stroked it. She knew he liked that, and she felt his eyes on her as he tilted his head back and breathed heavily.

Prudence began to slide down his body now, until she

was kneeling in front of him, and began to unfasten his breeches.

"You do not have to do this."

She looked up at him, her lips curling into a smile. "I know," she said. "But I want to."

He groaned as she leaned in and swept her tongue over him, trying to mimic the way he would sometimes use his mouth on her. His hand came to the back of her head, but only to gently cup it, not to force her to do anything or move in any way she did not initiate on her own.

"Prudence," he hissed as she made her way up to his crown, and then when she took the tip of him within her mouth and his knees shuddered in front of her, her own reaction shocked her as she began to throb in need for him.

"You are beautiful," he said, and she brought her fist to where his cock met his body, where she couldn't quite reach with her mouth. She felt rather clumsy as she moved back and forth, but he seemed to be enjoying what she was doing, if the way he moaned and moved in front of her was any indication.

She began to use her tongue on him, and that was when it all changed. He moved, harder, faster, until he yanked himself out of her mouth and was then determinately lifting her skirts.

They didn't make it to the bed, neither of them took their clothes off, and Prudence's skirts seemed to be flying about around her as he pushed into her. Prudence was already wet and ready for him, and she let out a moan that was near to a scream as he filled her completely. Prudence could hardly believe that by bringing him pleasure she was already so close to her own.

She felt the change in their lovemaking, realizing that before, he had always been somewhat gentle with her, treating her almost like a priceless doll. But now he seemed to be so close to the brink that he held nothing back, pulling out and sinking back into her with reckless abandon, and it made her hungrier for him than she had ever been before.

She pulled her knees back, allowing him the deepest access possible, as he lifted in and out of her faster now, until she began to pulse around him as she came while he groaned in her ear as the wood beneath her head and wool of the rug beneath her body bit into her back through the thin fabric of the muslin dress she wore.

"Prudence!" Benedict cried, and she felt the pulse grow within her – but it wasn't coming from her. It was him, as he was filling her with his seed, coming inside of her as he continued to thrust his hips.

Then he stopped, scrambling backward as he pulled out of her, leaving her there on the floor before him.

"I'm sorry," he said, and Prudence frowned at him, disappointed that those would be the first words to come out of his mouth.

"Don't be," she said, even as he walked to the side of the room, finding a piece of linen for her before bending and cleaning her up. She watched him, as uncertain about what he was feeling as he likely was. She could see the tightening of his jaw, feel the agitation radiating off him.

"Benedict," she said, reaching out and wrapping her hand around his arm before he could walk away from her. "Do not be upset about this. It happened. The chance that I am with child is low, and even if I am, then we will figure this out together. For we are married and are both perfectly capable of being good parents. I know it might not be what you wanted, but we will find our way through. Together."

He didn't quite meet her eyes as he nodded, and she could tell there was more that he was holding back from her, more reason that he didn't want to have a child with her besides that he didn't feel he was fit to be a father. Yet still, after all she had given and confessed to him, he still didn't trust her.

She straightened her dress, standing so that they were on equal footing. She was done with all the unspoken words and secrets between them. "I wanted to tell you that I loved you because I need you to understand where I am coming from when I ask you what I need to ask you."

"Which is what?" he said, turning around with arms crossed, staring at her.

She took a breath. Now was not the time for cowardice. "Why did you not tell me that my father was the man who ruined your family?"

His expression didn't change as he stared at her, his arms still crossed as he leaned back against the wall, his eyes shuttering.

"Does it matter?"

"Obviously it does if you didn't tell me."

"Does it make you suspect me of murder?"

She hated this eery tone his voice had taken on, one devoid of any emotion, including anger.

"No!" she exclaimed. "I defended you to them, told them that you could have nothing to do with my father's death or any threat to our family."

"Why would you think that?" he asked, tilting his head to the side, and for the first time, Prudence felt a slight twinge of fear. Why wasn't he denying it? Agreeing with her? Explaining the truth to her?

"Because I *know* you," she said, holding her hands out toward him in supplication. "I know that you would never do something like that."

"Because why?"

"Because!" Prudence said, wanting to stomp her foot on the ground in frustration, but knew that wouldn't help anything. "Because you are... you. And even though you are grumpy and surly, you have kindness within you, and you have always done the right thing when called upon. Because I have seen the way you love. Because I know, even if you refuse to admit it, that you love me as much as I love you."

She was breathing heavily when she finished, her heart racing as she had poured out everything that was within her to him, left it all waiting for him to step all over. And he simply stared at her.

"You think you know more than you do, Prudence," he finally said quietly, and her back stiffened at the lack of emotion in his words.

"You are trying to keep yourself away from me," she said, pointing a finger toward him.

"I do not love you. I cannot love you."

Prudence felt the pang in her heart at that, but she refused to respond. "Now you are lying."

"I am not."

"You are!" she exclaimed, hating that there were tears now escaping her eyes, threatening to run down her face in an increasing torrent, but she felt as though she had nothing left to give, while he refused to provide her anything in return. "Why can you not admit the truth?"

"Prudence, your family destroyed mine. I hated your father. Hated him. With everything that was within me. I hate your brother. The Remington name. The Remington family. I hated *you*."

Prudence blinked as rapidly as she could, but there was no preventing the tears now as she wondered what had happened to the man who had made love to her moments ago, who this was staring back at her now with no emotion, no compassion, nothing but vengeance on his mind and his face.

"How can you say that?" she asked, her voice cracking. "Why are you being so cruel?"

"This is who I am. I told you that from the very start. I have no idea why it would be such a surprise."

"It is *not* who you are!" she countered, stubbornly, venomously. "You are better than this. Inside, you are a good man. I know you are. I have seen you love. And as much as you might want to pretend otherwise, I know that you feel *something* for me. You would not make love to me so tenderly, would not walk me through Mayfair, would not be upset that I was fencing with another man if you didn't."

"I come to your bed because it feels good for me. I walk you through Mayfair so all know that you belong to me. And I am upset when you are with another man because it makes me look like a fool."

"Stop!" she said, her hand flinging toward him as she lashed out at him, but he caught her wrist.

"I did not kill your father," he said, finally saying something that she believed. "But I was happy to see him dead. And while I would never physically hurt you, nor anyone in your family, I will see to the downfall of the Remingtons myself. That I can promise you. Now, do what you have been waiting to do since you arrived," he said, his voice hard. "Take your daydreams and leave."

And at that, with all of the fight sucked out of her at Benedict's final words, Prudence turned around and fled.

CHAPTER 21

*P*rudence was halfway down the staircase when she realized that she was fleeing her own room, that leaving now meant doing so without any of her own possessions – but at this point, she no longer cared. All that mattered was to run, as fast as she was able.

For gone was the rational, practical Prudence, who thought she understood what everyone was thinking and feeling, that she knew better than what someone was saying to her face.

She had been so sure, so convinced that Benedict loved her as she loved him, despite the fact that he had not only never said the words to her, but he had told her again and again that he was not capable of doing so.

Then, finally, he had lashed out with his words, strongly enough that she truly had no choice but to believe him.

For how could a man treat a woman he loved in such a way?

He could not have made it more clear that he had absolutely meant what he said, that he had no love or desire for her, that she had been a complete fool to not only fall in love with him but to tell him so, to make herself vulnerable before him, in both body and mind.

Now she was running down the stairs as though he was chasing her, pausing just long enough to find her cloak and gloves. She knew she must look a fright, thoroughly disheveled from their lovemaking – if one could call it that – with her hair out of its pins, her face tear-stained, her dress barely fastened. Thank goodness she had, at least, kept her clothing on.

Jefferson, who likely had been overseeing the dinner preparations at this hour of the evening, began to stride toward her down the hall, but she lifted a quick hand to him.

"I'm leaving."

"I shall call the carriage, it will—"

"No."

"My lady, I—"

"I'm leaving *now*. Farewell, Jefferson, and thank you for everything."

Before he could protest once more, Prudence slammed the door behind her and ran out into the darkness.

With each step she took away from the house, the harder it was to keep her tears at bay, and she had just made it to the square in front of the townhouse when the first of her heavy sobs escaped. There were passersby, but it was dark enough that she didn't think anyone could make her out.

And even if they did, what did it matter? There would be scandal enough when all learned that she had left Benedict and their marriage. For she most certainly would not be going back to him. Not when he had treated her as he had, without any hint of remorse or understanding.

Prudence hated that she had to return to Warwick House, especially now after she had defended Benedict to her brother and the rest of her family. If there was one thing she despised, it was being played for a fool, and here they had been right the entire time. She, apparently, knew nothing and she never, ever should have agreed to this marriage, no matter what scandal ensued for her or for her family.

They had been through enough. They could have gotten through that too.

Now she had lost not only her pride but her heart as well, and she wasn't sure that she would ever be able to recover from it.

"Idiot," she muttered to herself as she kicked at a rock, becoming increasingly annoyed when the rock refused to move and worse, she managed to bruise her toe through her boot.

She pulled in a breath as she tried to consider just where Benedict's hatred had come from. She knew her father was not a good man, that he cared nothing for others but used people as required. Yet, she had thought he wouldn't have gone as far as to ruin another man for his own amusement.

Apparently, she had been wrong, and in the process, Benedict had lost everything that truly mattered.

Even so, she could not understand how he thought that ruining her entire family would right all the wrongs committed against him. Her father was dead. Prudence still believed that it had not been by Benedict's hand, but what did she know anymore? And what did it matter?

She was so intent on her own melancholy and analyzing how it had all come to this point that she didn't see the person in front of her until it was too late, and she ran into someone with enough speed that they both had to take a step backward.

"My apologies," she murmured. "I wasn't watching where I was going."

The person nodded but said nothing, which caused Prudence to look up to try to better ascertain just who she had bumped into – but found that the person wore a hat pulled down low and a cloak that covered just what type of attire was beneath.

She couldn't even tell if it was a man or a woman. Prudence was slightly taller of the two of them; however, she was taller than many men, so that didn't say much of anything.

Prudence took a step to the side to walk around, but the person stepped sideways, blocking her. Prudence let out a very unladylike growl, but the truth was, she had no time for this. Not tonight.

"Ex*cuse* me," she said, and at the lack of response, she tried to go around again, but this time when she did something hit the back of her head and she let out a groan as she sank to her knees, taking deep breaths while pain and bright lights exploded through her skull.

"What the—" she muttered, her panic urging her to regain her footing, to try to shake away the pain and get her bearings, but it was difficult to do so when it seemed as though her head was going to implode on itself.

Then the stranger in front of her stepped out of the way although didn't completely leave, while whoever must have attacked her was bending down toward her, lifting her up and over his shoulder as she was still too weak to fight him. This was a man, of that she was certain, although she couldn't make out anything about him either, not in the late evening darkness nor with the coverings upon him.

Prudence took another breath as she attempted to calm herself as her father had always taught her. There was always a way out, a defense, a parry, one that her opponent would not see coming if she timed it right.

She might not have the strength to fight this pair off, but she had more skill than they likely realized, as well as a weapon. One that she hadn't removed when she had met Benedict in the bedroom.

She lifted her hand as slowly as she could, having to wrench her arm back behind her to try to find what she was looking for. Reaching into the hidden pocket of her gown, she wrapped her hand around the comforting, familiar hilt of the blade, and then lifted it in her hand as she tried to decide what to do.

Prudence had no desire to kill the man, but nor did she want him to have any ability to come after her once more.

She lifted her dagger hand as slowly and surreptitiously as she could, and then brought the blade down into the man's shoulder, between his collarbone and shoulder blade.

He let out a howl as he dropped her, and Prudence threw herself into a ball as she landed on the ground. She grunted as her shoulder still took a fair bit of her weight, but she was able to roll out of the way before the second attacker could come after her.

"You idiot!" she heard the first person shout at the man she had injured as she took off running as fast as she could, thankful that she hadn't fallen on an ankle. She gasped in pain as something sharp and heavy caught her in the back as she ran, and she gritted her teeth to continue through its bite as she realized with incredulity that one of them was throwing rocks at her.

"Get her!" came the next scream, which caused Prudence to continue to churn her legs more quickly as she became grateful for all the training she had done that allowed her such endurance and the ability to run faster than most women, despite the skirts that impeded her.

It was only when she had finally escaped them that she realized the second voice had not been a man's – but a woman's. And it was a familiar one.

If Prudence could just remember where she had heard it before.

* * *

BENEDICT SAT in his dark mahogany chair in front of his desk, a place that usually brought him such solace.

But not tonight.

He had waved away the dinner that a footman had attempted to deliver, for he had no appetite whatsoever. In fact, he thought if he took a bite of food, he would be likely to lose it but moments later.

For he was absolutely disgusted with himself.

He sank his head into his hands, as suddenly it seemed too heavy to hold up with his neck alone.

It didn't matter whether he closed his eyes or left them open – all he could see was the pain on Prudence's face as he had told her that he didn't love her, that he was using her, that he hated both her and her family.

He had thought he had reached the lowest point in his life before, when he had lost both of his parents. But now, he had also lost the one thing, the one *person* who had ever made him feel better since their demise.

What made it worse this time was that there was no one else he could blame. It had all been entirely his own doing.

He knew he never should have given her any reason to love him. He never should have invited her into his bed, or showed her any compassion, or any inkling that he was even capable of loving another.

But somehow, it had happened whether he had meant it to or not, and despite his best efforts, she had grown to love him even when she should have continued her hatred of him.

He never should have married her.

He should have thrown her out of his study as soon as he had seen her within it – before there had been any opportunity for another to find them together.

Now he would be forever tied to her in name. And heart. And body. And mind.

The words he had said to her were unforgiveable.

Untrue, but unforgiveable.

He could but imagine what her brother was saying to her now – that he had warned her not to return to him, that he was likely not only a terrible man but a killer as well. Benedict guessed that it wouldn't be long now until he was once more being accused of the duke's murder, of being the man threatening the Remington family. For now they had additional reason to hate him, and he had all but told Prudence that he would be responsible for their demise. While he didn't mean that literally, how could it not be considered a confession?

The worst of it was that she was right – he did love her, really and truly, and he had thrown that love away. For no matter what happened now, he could never take back his words. They were inexcusable, and he could do no more than hope that Prudence finally realized the truth.

She was too good for him. She was better off without him, and she should run as far and as fast from him as she possibly could.

CHAPTER 22

*P*rudence ran until she could run no more, hoping she was moving in the right direction.

But when she finally stopped, certain that she had left behind whoever was chasing her, she realized that she was likely in a worse situation than when she had started.

For she had no idea where she was.

She wasn't in Mayfair – she had known that when the streets began to smell fouler, when the buildings around her had somewhat deteriorated, when the greenery that bordered the pathways became unkept and untrimmed.

The problem was, she had not ventured this way often before, and now she was completely turned around, it was dark, and she had no idea just who she could trust to ask for directions or to at least provide her an idea of where she was.

She stumbled as her head throbbed, though she was fairly certain that it wasn't a severe injury or else she would have been in greater distress. Whoever had attacked her must not have been knowledgeable of what he was doing, which led her to believe that this was someone who had never acted in such a way before.

She had recognized Regent Street when she had crossed it so she figured she must be in Soho, which was not the *worst* place to be; it was just that she had no idea how she was going to make it back to where she had started.

"You looking for someone?" came a voice to her right, and she started, placing a hand on her heart. She had never been this woman who jumped at every shadow around her, but then, she had also never been in such a situation before – always wondering where the next threat to her family was going to come from.

She hesitated, her hand on the now-bloody dagger that was back in her pocket, but when she looked up, she saw that the man was accompanied by a woman, their arms inter-twined, and, if anything, the light from the building behind her was cast upon faces that seemed concerned rather than threatening.

"My brother," Prudence said, hearing the raggedness of her own breathing. "I was trying to find him in Mayfair, but I got lost."

"You have certainly been moving in the wrong direction for a time, then," the woman said, lines of concern creasing her forehead. "Turn around the way you came. Depending on where in Mayfair you are going, you will want to go right or left at Regent Street. It is a fair walk, however. Would you not prefer a hack?"

She looked Prudence up and down, obviously realizing that Prudence's clothing was of fine quality, although it was at complete odds with how she must look now after all she had been through tonight. If she had been dishevelled before, now she must look a fright – although how she looked and the pain in her shoulder, head, and back had nothing on the pain Benedict had inflicted upon her heart.

"I'm fine," she said, attempting to force a smile on her face. "Thank you so much."

She turned away from their worried expressions and back down the street, hoping that she would be able to find home.

Prudence kept her head down as she walked, her shoulders hunched, and her senses wary. She was prepared for anything that might come at her, unsure if she should be relieved or on edge as she approached Mayfair and all around her became much more familiar. For· it was in Mayfair where the threat had seemed to lie, and here where she knew with a growing sense of certainty that her family would soon discover who was against them. She could only hope they all emerged from this unscathed.

Despite all her training, she was weary by the time she neared Warwick House, and she nearly stumbled in front of a residence all too familiar. She dragged herself to the doorstep of the home that had become secondary to her own home, hoping against hope that its resident would be there.

When Hugo opened the doorway, she all but fell into his arms.

"Prudence!" he exclaimed, catching her as he helped her into the room. "Good heavens, what happened to you?"

It wasn't until he had seated her on the sofa in his small living area that she realized he wasn't alone. She saw two drinks on the table before her, and she looked around to see who else might be there.

"Hugo, I'm so sorry. You have company. I should go, I—"

"Sit down this instant," he said, pointing a finger at her. "And talk."

"But—"

"Prudence, you look like you've been through hell. You are not going anywhere. It's fine. He retired to the other room as he is not comfortable with anyone knowing his identity. Give me a moment to explain, and I shall return."

Prudence sank her head into her hands as she watched

Hugo walk across the room, open the door, murmur a few soft words, and then return.

"Now," he said, passing her his own cup, which contained a strong-smelling alcohol. "Talk."

And so she did. She poured out her heart to the man who had provided her all the support she would ever need over the last number of years, who had been there for her when no one else could have understood. He listened without interrupting, although she could see the emotion playing out on his face when she told him exactly what Benedict had said. When she finished, he leaned back, interlacing his fingers around his knee.

"Oh, Prudence," he said with a sigh. "This is certainly a conundrum."

"Yes," she said, "for I am married to him, and that cannot be changed."

"Unless he is the one who killed your father and will now be hanged for it."

"Hugo!"

"Would you want that?"

Prudence looked down at her hands. She should – especially if Benedict was guilty. And yet—

"No," she said, her voice hardly above a whisper. "I would not."

"Well, then, you have a lot to contemplate regarding your marriage, but perhaps that should come later," he said. "Right now, the most important thing is to keep you safe, or else there will be nothing to worry about at a later time. We need to return you to Warwick House to tell your family all that has occurred. This has got to end. Thank God you can take care of yourself. Are you certain that you are not injured?"

"I'll be fine," she said, though she winced when she lifted her hand to the back of her skull, wondering just what they had hit her with. "Thank you for being here, Hugo."

"Of course," he said. "Now, let's get you to Warwick House and end this once and for all."

* * *

AFTER HUGO HELPED her clean up enough that she wouldn't completely terrify her family when she walked through the front door of the Warwick mansion, the two of them made their way to what had been home to Prudence for most of her life.

But as she walked up the familiar steps, a strange sense of unease overcame her – one that made her feel displaced, as though there was nowhere that she truly belonged anymore.

She shook it off, however, for at the moment, she had greater problems to deal with.

"Prudence?"

Emma was the first one she saw, who the butler, Jameson, must have called once she and Hugo had entered the front door. The moment she saw her, Emma rushed toward her with concern.

"What has happened?"

"Perhaps we should all sit down," Hugo said, and Emma looked to him with a nod. Prudence knew that Emma didn't know Hugo overly well, but she would be aware that he was a close friend of the family's, especially of Prudence. They had grown up together in the country, but Giles had been away for most of the time they would have spent together, in addition to being a few years older than Hugo.

Giles walked into the room, stopping abruptly when he saw Prudence.

"What the hell happened? I swear if Trundelle hurt you—"

"He didn't," Prudence said, holding up a hand, though she modified her answer slightly when Hugo gave her a look.

"Well, not physically. But we will speak of my marriage later. Our first concern is what happened *after* I left home."

He nodded and sent a note around for Matthew to join them. After Hugo imparted the information that Prudence had been injured, he also sent for Hudson, and it wasn't long until they had all gathered once more – including Lady Winchester, who had come down to see what all the fuss was about.

After ensuring that Prudence was looked after and in good hands, Hugo left, likely back to his company, Prudence thought with a small smile, glad that he, at least, was happy.

Prudence began the story with her attack, which caused them all great concern, but it was Giles who asked the first question.

"Why were you walking around London alone after dark, Prudence?" he asked, anger growing on his face before he even had the answer to his question, and Prudence had to swallow the lump in her throat as well as the instinct to defend Benedict. For why would she do so any longer?

"Benedict and I... had an argument," she said. "A falling out, if you will."

"About what?"

"I confronted him about what you told me regarding his past and our suspicions. He... he admitted to all of it, and in the end said that I was best without him. That he hated our family for everything Father had done to him, and that he would ruin us in the end."

Giles began pacing up and down the room. "I knew it," he muttered.

"But Giles," Prudence said as she stood, her hands on her hips. "He seemed to be more concerned with ruining our family in another sense, not to actually kill or injure any of us. And why would I be attacked *after* I had left his house?"

"Because it would be too obvious if he did anything to you there."

"Yes, but there is something else," she said, rubbing the back of her head as she thought on it. "Two people attacked me, and one of them, I swear, was a woman. There are no other women in Benedict's life, no one else who would help him with such a thing. Certainly not his aunt or sister-in-law."

"How can you be sure it was a woman?" Giles asked, stopping his pacing and staring at her.

"Her voice," Prudence said, frowning. "And it seemed a familiar one."

Giles ran a hand through his hair as he turned around.

"He was to take care of you, and he let you out into the night. Alone."

Prudence opened her mouth to defend Benedict — it had been her own foolish decision to leave — but it was their grandmother who stood now and commanded their attention.

"That does it," she said, thumping her cane on the ground. "Your husband has a lot to say for himself, Prudence, but I agree with you – he isn't the one we need to be worried about."

"Then who?" Giles said, lifting his hands out to the side.

"Stay here," Lady Winchester said, pointing her cane at him. "I will be back in a moment. In the meantime, have Lewis treat that poor girl's head. I can see the blood in her hair from here."

"I suspect Lady Winchester and I have come to the same conclusion," Matthew murmured, before following her from the room with Giles trailing after them.

After exchanging bewildered glances and knowing there was nothing they could do but wait, Prudence sat down with

Emma, Juliana, and Maria, as Hudson stood behind her discretely and began to look at her injuries.

"As for Benedict," Emma began, "I am not sure what to tell you, Pru. When I saw the two of you together, I could have sworn that that man loved you, truly I could have."

"I thought the same," Prudence said morosely. "Yet here we are."

"But the way he looks at you..." Emma continued, staring off into the distance, and Prudence shrugged.

"I suppose that was all part of his plan."

"But how could he have planned that you would enter his house, that you would be found in a compromising position, that Giles would encourage you to marry him?" Emma protested.

"Perhaps once the opportunity presented itself, he decided to take advantage," Juliana added, and Prudence closed her eyes, wishing they were speaking of another's marriage and not her own.

"Or..." Maria said softly, and they all looked to her, for Maria wasn't always the first to speak, but when she did, it was usually because she had thought long and hard and had wisdom to impart. "He could be hurting. Truly, deeply hurting from his past, and he just doesn't know how to love or how to allow someone to love him. You told him how you felt for him, Prudence?"

Prudence nodded as she blinked back the tears that threatened once more.

"Then perhaps it scared him, and he pushed you away even before realizing exactly what he was doing."

"Perhaps you're right," Prudence said, biting her lip, wincing slightly as Hudson pressed his hand against the back of her head.

"You have a fairly sizeable bump, but it is reassuring, actually, that it swelled this way instead of the other," he said.

"As you can move your shoulder, I would assume that it and the welt on your back will produce some bruising, but you should be fine and have no issues with mobility."

Prudence nodded, thanking him as her grandmother re-entered the room, Matthew and Giles following her somewhat sheepishly.

"Well, I have had some time to think and now, with what you have told me, Prudence, I am certain," she said, lifting her chin and tapping her cane against the ground. "I know who killed Warwick and is after our family. And I have a plan for just what, exactly, we are going to do about it."

CHAPTER 23

*B*enedict stayed awake all night.

He did nothing but sit in front of the fire, considering his life and all the choices that had led him to this point. Some he had made himself, although most others had been made for him, in one way or another.

There had been but a few years in his life when he hadn't known loss.

And it was odd, even though he had been closer to the Remington family — the people he had thought he had despised more than any other — than he had ever been before he had married Prudence, in the last two months he had felt the most whole than he ever had.

Until he had lost it all once more.

There was a knock on his study door, and Benedict shifted in his chair as he blinked his eyes to try to determine what time the mantel clock was showing, but it appeared too blurry for him to actually make anything out.

He did recall being offered breakfast and then a second meal, so he supposed it must be mid-afternoon.

"What is it?" he asked, hearing the hoarseness of his voice, realizing that all he'd consumed since Prudence had left had been whiskey.

"You have visitors, my lord," came Jefferson's voice, and Benedict was tempted to throw something at the door.

"Tell them I am not in," he said, knowing that the only people who might be visiting him at the moment were Martin and Amelia or Aunt Emily. He supposed it could also be Remington, here to kill him for hurting his sister.

"They are not taking no for an answer, my lord," Jefferson's voice echoed again, except this time the door swung open, to reveal, sure enough, Remington standing in the doorway, with Hugo Conway, Prudence's mysterious friend, standing behind him.

Ah, so this might be his end, then. So be it.

Remington's face was tight with anger, while Conway looked altogether dismayed.

"What, then, are you challenging me to a duel?" he said, as he allowed the smirk he so often wore to cross his face, hoping that it would mask what he was truly feeling. "I assure you I have done no damage to Prudence's honor."

"Do not say her name, you son of a bitch," Remington bit out, which caused Benedict to stand, although he had to keep a hand on the back of his chair in order to stay upright, and he wondered if he would, in fact, be able to even compete in a duel in his current condition. And then there was the question, from a small voice in the back of his mind, whether he even wanted to.

"I told her from the start that there could never be love between us," he said, shrugging. "I warned her."

"Whatever you said, it sent her out into the night. Alone. For her to be attacked."

"What?" That sobered Benedict quicker than anything else ever could. "You're lying."

"I am not. Tell him, Conway."

Conway stepped into the room beside Remington, folding his arms over his chest as he also stared at Benedict, although he seemed less angry and more contemplative.

"It's the truth. She was attacked."

"Is she hurt?"

"Why do you care?" Remington asked, incredulity in his words.

"I think he cares more than we realize, Remington," Conway said. "Look at him. Doesn't appear the man has slept."

"Go away. Both of you," was all Benedict could manage. "After you tell me if Prudence is all right."

"She is—" Conway began, but Remington interrupted him.

"You do not deserve to know."

"I did nothing!" Benedict cried out in frustration.

"You told me that you would look after her. That, if nothing else, you would keep her safe. You failed, and I will never forgive you for that. Hell, I will never forgive myself. I never should have allowed this marriage to happen."

"Never should have pushed it, you mean," Benedict said, unable to help himself, noting that Remington began to ball his hands into fists.

Conway stepped in between them. "This is enough. I believe we are all concerned for Prudence, and yes, this began with your words toward her, Trundelle, but perhaps we can come to some conclusion, no? May we sit?"

Benedict opened his mouth to tell them no, but decided it was best to be done with this and then he could have all the Remingtons out of his life for good. He waved to the rarely used chairs in front of his desk and the two unlikely paired men took a seat.

"We all know the story now of your past with the former Duke of Warwick," Conway began, obviously determining that he had to be the mediator of this meeting. "Since then, you have built up your fortune and, in the process, have brought down men who were associated with Remington's father. Would you like to explain this?"

Benedict leaned forward. "No."

"Why did you marry my sister?" Remington asked instead, causing Conway to roll his eyes as he apparently realized this conversation was not going to go as he planned.

"Because I was promised that she wanted nothing to do with me, that, despite being married to avoid scandal, we would continue to live separate lives," he said with a shrug. "And also, I was always taught to keep your enemies closer than your friends."

"Until she came *too* close," Conway said softly. "And then you pushed her away."

Benedict couldn't meet his eyes, as the truth of the man's words began to sink deeply into his chest. Yet these were the last men he wanted to admit such a thing to.

"She wouldn't understand."

"Understand what?" Conway continued to push.

"That she is too good for me! That I will only hurt her all the worse once this ends."

"And just how do you suppose this is all going to end?" Remington asked, leaning forward, his elbows on his knees. "Why do you not just tell me how you plan to ruin me, and I will save you the trouble of whatever you have planned? For I can tell you, Trundelle, many people hated my father, and I was on that long list of people. I'm trying to rebuild our family, our name. The truth is, I can understand why you would have hated him as well. But why can we not move forward together, and not be stuck in the past? If you do have any feelings for my sister besides this hatred for my family – and from the look of you, I suppose Conway is right, and it is likely that you do – then let us figure this out without ruining anyone else and putting my sister's life in danger."

"Is she—"

"She is fine. Hurt but fine."

Benedict sat back, taking a deep breath. He had started this all with one goal, which had been bringing down the Remington family. Then somehow, through it all, a new priority had emerged – to keep Prudence safe. And in his blindness, he had failed miserably. Remington had every reason to hate him, but he didn't have to, for now Benedict hated himself as much as anyone else ever could. At this point, telling Remington of his scheme would not hurt either of them, for there was nothing stopping him from going ahead with his plan – except himself.

He lifted his head and finally met Remington's eye.

"Very well," he said, before leaning back to begin his tale. "I may have been young when my father died, but I never forgot the events leading up to his death – nor my mother's. Once I finished school and was old enough to fully assume the role of earl, I made it my first order of business to discover just *how* Warwick had ruined him."

He could tell by the way Remington was staring at him that the man actually didn't know much himself about his father's actions. Interesting.

"Your father had devised a scheme in which he convinced other members of the *ton* to invest their money with him. However, it was all a sham, and there was nothing to actually invest into. By the time the men realized they had been played, it was too late. It was fraud at its highest level, but everyone involved was too ashamed to go to the authorities about it, or to admit their own foolishness to any other. I, however, had no such shame. Not anymore."

"So why did you never tell anyone?" Remington asked, leaning forward.

"I did something better. I went to the duke himself, told him that I knew all, and that I had evidence. He offered to buy my silence. I agreed to what he said, although I had no intention of keeping my promise. Instead, I allowed him to think that he had my allegiance, and I used information he provided me to blackmail friends of his, slowly buying up vowels so that I could bring down the worst of them when they least expected it. When I cashed in, they were provided one other option – to help me build evidence against the duke. And many of them did. I was nearly ready to strike when Warwick very inconveniently died. Unfortunately for you, Remington, that meant you inherited my vendetta against him along with the title. Dennison had thought we were in league together against you, but he truly had nothing on you but imaginary vowels. When I realized the sort of man he truly was, I had already decided to ruin him, but then he also died before I could."

The two visitors regarded him with some incredulity, and a few moments of silence ticked by before Remington leaned forward once more.

"How interesting that the men you vow to bring down continue to so inconveniently die on you."

Benedict nodded. "I agree."

"So what were you going to do now with all this evidence that you have, apparently, accumulated?"

Benedict paused for a moment, wondering himself just what he was going to do next. He had thought everything was so straightforward, but his plans were slowly changing before him.

"I had planned to bring the information forward in the House of Lords. I have quite a case. And then it would be up to you to provide restitution to everyone your father wronged."

"I cannot be held guilty for another man's sins – even if he was my father, whether I wanted him to be or not."

"That is true," Benedict agreed. "But your estate holds money that is illegally yours."

Remington crossed one leg over the other, tapping his foot up and down.

"And now?"

"Now I am not sure what I am going to do," Benedict admitted.

Conway looked back and forth between the two of them before clearing his throat.

"If I may... it seems to be that both of you have had great wrongs done to you. My question is, how does continuing to aggrieve one another put either of you any further ahead? And at the end of this all, who is the one left truly hurt?"

Prudence.

Benedict groaned and ran a hand over his face.

"So what are we to do now?"

"You are to come to a conclusion that benefits both of you. Then continue living your lives with the women you love and the family that you have inherited in one another."

Benedict looked up, meeting Hugo's eyes, realizing that the three of them in this room loved Prudence more than any other men ever could, each of them in their own way.

"She will never forgive me," he said, his words barely louder than a whisper.

"There is just one way to determine that for certain," Conway said. "You have to give it a try."

CHAPTER 24

*P*rudence had finally listened to Hudson's advice and taken to bed in what had once been her room. She had barely started any of the work she had planned to update Benedict's house, and she wondered if he had even noticed anything had changed.

Here at Warwick House, all remained the same. Was she going to just fall back into the life she had left behind, where nothing would be different but her name and title? At least, if nothing else, she could still be Peter Robertson when she chose. It was the one piece of her that she still had for herself, although she was unsure if she would ever be able to fence again without thinking of Benedict.

Benedict. She would have to return and face him at some point in time, to collect all of her possessions and leave once more, but it was too soon for her to see him again. She would likely break down before him, and that was the last thing she would allow herself to do.

"Prudence?"

The knock on her door startled her, as did most things at the moment. She needed a good fencing bout, she considered. If she had been at home, she and Benedict– But no, she couldn't think like that. That small part of her life was finished now, and she had to move on.

Perhaps Giles would fence with her. She knew he was rather rusty, but what better way to improve than to return to the sport? If he refused, she could always find Hugo, although she still felt slightly guilty for interrupting him last night.

"Who's there?" she mumbled and was shocked when the door opened slightly and the last person that she ever expected was standing in its opening. "Benedict?"

"Prudence," he said, stepping into the room, closing the door behind him, although he made no effort to take another step forward, as though he was ready to escape quickly should he be required to do so. "I knew if I was announced you likely wouldn't see me."

Prudence's emotions quickly changed from surprise to thrilled to now anger once more.

"You are correct. I have no wish to see you. In fact, I would prefer that you leave. How could you stand to be in the presence of a woman you hate, anyway?"

"I never should have said that," said Benedict as he slowly moved forward.

"But it was true, was it not?" she asked, trying to push herself higher on the bed once more so that she wouldn't be looking up at him.

He sighed as he sat down on the mattress of the bed, surprising her with his temperament, for no longer did he appear to be the challenging opponent that he always presented to the world.

"I will not lie and say that I never hated you," he said, and Prudence crossed her arms over her chest in defense of herself. "But that was before I knew you."

"You told me but *yesterday* that you hated me. I hardly

think anything would have changed since then, nor is it fair to judge someone before having ever even met them."

"I know," he said, leaning forward and running his hands through his hair – hair that Prudence now knew nearly as well as her own, that, despite everything that had happened, she longed to feel again.

"Prudence, I have to know – are you all right? I heard that you were attacked and I—and I—"

Prudence leaned forward. Was he truly choking on his words?

"I'm fine," she said, refusing to allow her heart to soften toward him. "What is this, Benedict? Is it all an act? Some game that you are playing to make me believe that you have no more ill intentions toward me? I find it hard to believe that everything has changed in but one day."

"I was just trying to keep from hurting you," he said, and Prudence snorted.

"Well, you did a lousy job of it, for I can assure you that you hurt me very, very much. Do you know what it is like to tell someone that you love him, only to have him throw it back in your face? I never expected you to tell me the same, but at the very least, I was hoping that you could show some form of affection toward me. But no, you did the exact opposite."

"Prudence, I—"

"Save it," she said, throwing her hands in the air. "I do not want to hear it."

"I do love you," he muttered, and Prudence was torn as she so desperately wanted to believe what he was saying, yet how could she? Since the moment she had met him, he had continued to say one thing and act in a completely different manner entirely. Now he was saying what she wanted to hear, but how could she possibly believe him?

"Your words are not enough," she said, shaking her head. "For I do not trust you. Not anymore."

She would not put her heart out for him to break again, for she didn't think she could bear it another time.

He folded his hands in front of him before standing and nodding to her.

"I know what I said to you is unforgiveable, so I understand your feelings. And you're right – you are too good for me, and I have no expectation for you to return to me. But I wanted you to know… that you did not deserve the words I threw at you, and that you are the best woman I have ever known. If you ever need anything from me, Prudence, I shall be there for you. That, I can promise you."

Prudence nodded stiffly but didn't say anything else, for she didn't trust herself to speak without sobbing. She still loved him, with all her heart, despite all that he had said to her, but she had learned her lesson of what came with putting that love out into the world.

He had been right from the start. It was too difficult to share that love. It was better to keep it within.

She was strong. She was powerful. She could do this.

Except, as he left, shutting the door softly behind him, she melted into the bed, wondering if she would ever recover.

* * *

"IT DIDN'T QUITE GO as you expected, then?" Remington asked from behind the desk in his study, as Benedict sat morosely on the other side. After Prudence had told him what she was feeling for him, he hadn't gone far, for Remington had met him with a knowing look before he could exit the mansion.

"It went as I expected," he muttered. "She turned me away.

She doesn't trust me, never wants to see me again, doesn't believe in my words."

"Does she know what you did?"

"Give you all my evidence against your father? No." He shook his head. "Do not tell her. Please. She is right. She *is* better off without me."

He waited for Remington to agree, but before the man could say anything, the door opened to reveal Prudence's rather formidable grandmother.

"This is all utter nonsense, and you are both fools," she said, rolling her eyes. "Never thought I'd say that about Prudence. Figured she was the smart one. Not to worry – she will come around. Damn Warwick and all the sins he committed."

"Careful, Grandmother, or we will begin to believe that you were the one who killed him," Remington said wryly, but there was a hint of humor in his eyes.

Lady Winchester straightened. "If I had killed him, I would never have poisoned him. I would have stood in front of him so that I could watch him realize it was me who did it, see the light go out of his eyes at the end."

"Grandmother!"

She shrugged. "It's the truth." She focused on Benedict. "Now, you will eventually have to admit to Prudence what you did for her, but in the meantime, we have a murder to solve and must bring this all to an end. I have invited guests for dinner tonight."

"I hope you're not planning on poisoning anyone," Remington said, and his Grandmother walked farther into the room and swatted him with her cane. Suddenly, Benedict had a glimpse of what Prudence would be like in fifty years, and he wished with all his might that he would be with her to witness it.

"What did I just tell you? I would never choose poison. I would far prefer a duel."

"I would be very interested in seeing that," Benedict couldn't help but say, which earned him a raised brow that had him shivering slightly.

"While you will not be seeing it, I would suggest that you stay tonight as well, young man," she said. "You might have a role to play yet."

Benedict looked over to Remington, who shrugged in some bewilderment.

"We do not often disagree with her," he said, which had Benedict snorting once more. How could they all be so scared of an elderly woman?

He snuck a peek back at her, however, and realized that perhaps they were onto something. If he didn't know better, he would have thought that she could see right through him.

"What time is dinner?" he asked.

"In three hours," Lady Winchester said. "We shall see you soon. Do not blunder this."

Benedict nodded as Lady Winchester shut the door behind her.

"Is she always like that?" he asked Remington but was answered with an "I most certainly am!" from the hall, and he found himself doing something he hardly ever did: he chuckled.

Soon Remington chimed in, and before he knew it, they were laughing together.

Which was how Archibald and Lewis found them a short time later. They stood together in the doorway, looking at the two of them incredulously.

"Have the two of you been taking some kind of drug?" Lewis asked, and they managed to recover themselves.

"No," Remington replied to the physician, as his laugh slowly ebbed. "Come in. We have a lot to plan for tonight."

"Do you think we should speak with the women as well?" Lewis asked, to which Archibald grinned.

"They already have the plan in place. Do you not realize that we are simply there as accessories?" He chuckled slightly himself. "Juliana told me to be sure my men were available as backup, and that my job was to ensure that no one else was injured. Everything else, she assured me, would be taken care of."

Benedict looked between them all in bewilderment. "That is it? You are leaving this all up to the women?"

"Ah, Trundelle, it appears you have some learning to do yet," Remington said with a chagrined smile. "I had the benefit of sisters who taught me years ago that it was far easier to allow it to happen this way. Now, who needs a drink?"

It was the best decision they had made yet that day.

CHAPTER 25

*P*rudence perched on the edge of the sofa in the drawing room as they waited for the rest of their party to arrive. The men had yet to join them, and Juliana placed a hand on her knee.

"Stop fidgeting," she said. "You look more nervous than I feel."

"I cannot help it," Prudence returned. "I am far too on edge."

"You are the most capable of any of us," Juliana said, turning wide eyes on her. "How can you not feel prepared?"

"It is not as though I am sitting here with my sword in hand, prepared to duel."

"No, but I am sure you have a dagger on you somewhere."

Prudence tilted her head in agreement. "That is true."

"What happens now?" Emma asked, turning to their grandmother, who regally straightened her spine.

"We wait."

"Where is Mother?" Juliana asked, looking around the drawing room, and their grandmother shot her a look.

"She will be joining us any moment," Lady Winchester

said. "But remember, do not tell her any of our plan. She will never believe the truth until she hears it for herself."

They nodded in agreement as the door opened, and Prudence's heart jumped – but it was only her brother and her brothers-in-law. Then she saw who else had accompanied them.

Benedict didn't meet anyone's eyes as he entered the room, his shoulders held tight and tense as he walked toward her and took a seat next to her. Prudence rigidly held herself away from him, fighting with her own body, which wanted to lean into him and accept his comfort.

"What are you doing here?" she hissed under her breath.

"I wanted to be here for you," he said in a low voice. "In case you need me."

"I do not. I will not."

"I know, Prudence, I do," he said, looking down at his hands. "Your grandmother and your brother asked me to stay, so here I am. After tonight, after this is all over, I will be out of your life if that is what you choose. I promise."

He looked up at her then, and his eyes were so full of pain that she had to take a deep breath to steel her resolve. But then she reminded herself of everything he had said to her, everything he felt about her, and she gave a sharp nod and turned from him as her mother entered the room.

"How wonderful to see you all," she said, ever the gracious hostess. "We certainly have an… eclectic collection of guests tonight."

Of course her mother could never fully accept that Matthew, a detective, was now part of their family. And then there was the fact that Hudson was here. He might be a physician, but he was still the former duke's bastard son, and Prudence wondered if her mother would ever be able to overcome that fact, even though Hudson and Giles had formed a tentative friendship despite their rocky beginning.

She knew that Giles had offered to bring Hudson into society, but he had outright refused. Prudence didn't blame him.

The butler appeared in the doorway then. "Lord and Lady Hemingway have arrived."

"Oh, wonderful," her mother said, appearing relieved, likely because someone of her status had arrived with whom she could speak. "Do show them in."

The butler nodded as Lord Hemingway stepped into the room, followed by his mother, who appeared surprised to see them all gathered.

"I didn't realize there would be so many... guests tonight," she said, her gaze landing on Prudence and Benedict for an extra moment.

"Are we not fortunate to have such love and happiness within our family?" Lady Winchester said, clearly with forced sweetness. "Do have a seat."

"Thank you," Lady Hemingway said as the footmen began to bring in drinks for them all before they went in to dinner.

Her grandmother, however, did not sit, but instead remained in the middle of the room, commanding it.

"While gathering family is always one of the greatest joys, tonight we are all here for a special purpose," she said, her voice carrying as she was obviously enjoying the moment. "We have discovered who murdered the previous duke and has been threatening our family."

Lord Hemingway wore a shocked expression, while Lady Hemingway appeared to properly hide her emotion.

"Oh, thank goodness," Lady Hemingway said, bringing a hand to her breast. "Do tell us, who is it?"

"The murderer is within this very room," Lady Winchester said dramatically.

Lady Hemingway gasped. "But it is – mostly – family in this room," she said, turning her eyes on Benedict accusingly, and Prudence nearly rolled her eyes. "Should we not be frightened?"

"I do not see the point of such emotion," her grandmother said, "for a killer who would use poison to achieve their means would never have enough gumption to try anything in the light of day, now would they?"

"Perhaps we should just get to the point," Lord Hemingway said, standing as he nervously twisted his hands together – flinching as he pushed himself up from his seat.

"Very well, Lord Hemingway," Lady Winchester said. "What do you have to say for yourself?"

"Me?"

"Yes. Do you have any involvement in this?"

"Of course not," he said, his cheeks going red as he looked around the room. "How could you say such a thing? You know that I consider myself part of this family."

"You are not, though, in truth, are you?" her grandmother said, raising a brow, and Prudence considered that had her grandmother not been born into the nobility, she would have been made for the stage. "You are close to the family because of the friendship between your mother and the dowager duchess, and you are in line to inherit after Giles because, quite frankly, there is just no one else. But that came into question recently and will so again once Emma and Giles have another child."

"Unless they have all girls," Lady Hemingway interjected, and Lady Winchester raised a brow.

"Possible, but not likely," she said, "especially with the way these two are at one another all the time."

Emma's mouth dropped open, her cheeks turning scarlet, while the dowager duchess exclaimed, "Mother!" In horror.

But Prudence's grandmother didn't seem to care. She never had been particularly circumspect, and she certainly didn't appear to be starting such a course now.

"Continuing on," she said, walking over and poking her cane into Lord Hemingway's shoulder. He gasped in pain as he lifted his hand and gripped his apparent injury. "Lord Hemingway, are you going to admit to any involvement?"

"I—that is—"

"I see you are having trouble speaking. Well, as it is, I have called the magistrate to come and help us. The very same one that accompanied us when we thought we were going to need a witness for Lord Dennison's confession. Mr. Graham, you are welcome to come in."

Lord and Lady Hemingway turned horrified glances toward the man walking through the door.

"Now, Lord Hemingway, do tell us, why did you arrange for Prudence to be standing underneath the chandelier when it nearly fell atop her?"

"I—I didn't know that it was going to fall!" he stuttered, staring at Prudence with wide eyes and hands outstretched. "You have to believe me. I would never do anything to hurt you."

"Wouldn't you, though?" Lady Winchester said, cocking her head. "Were you not hoping her brother would come to her rescue and be caught beneath it instead? And what about hitting her in the back of the head?"

"I—it was not—it was only supposed to knock her out! But it didn't even do that!"

Prudence's eyes widened. She knew her grandmother was never usually wrong, but she'd had a difficult time believing that Lord Hemingway could actually be behind all that had happened.

He had the motivation, yes, but he was not particularly cunning, nor intelligent. Unless the bumbling character had all been an act that he had kept up for years.

"Do you need more of a confession, Mr. Graham?" Giles

asked. "Or perhaps first we should have Hemingway here admit that he killed my father."

"I didn't!" Lord Hemingway said, looking around at them all. "You must understand, I could never actually kill someone! Perhaps do a few small things to help my—" He stopped himself before going further.

"Your what?" Lady Winchester said.

"Nothing," Lord Hemingway said, his shoulders slouching. "Very well. Yes, I did it. I killed—"

"Shut your mouth!" Lady Hemingway stood now, hands in fists at her side as she glared at her son. "Stop talking, you idiot!"

Prudence's mouth dropped open. She knew that voice. And not just as Lady Hemingway's voice, but as one she recognized from having heard it in another setting entirely.

"Mother, I—"

"We had nothing to do with any of this!" she said shrilly. "We are leaving. I can hardly believe that you would treat us like this. Have you no shame? Elizabeth?"

She looked to Prudence's mother, who was sitting there wearing an expression of shock.

"I do not want to believe it," she said. "But Lord Hemingway just said—"

"He didn't know what he was saying," Lady Hemingway snapped, the look of anger and defiance on her face nastier than anything Prudence had seen before. "Come, son. We are leaving. We are obviously not wanted here."

"I'm afraid that we cannot allow you to leave," the magistrate said apologetically. "Lord Hemingway admitted to injuring Lady Prudence—"

"Lady Trundelle," Benedict growled from beside her.

"Lady Trundelle," Graham corrected. "And for positioning her beneath a chandelier he knew would fall."

"I never knew it would fall!" Lord Hemingway

proclaimed, and they all turned to him as Giles stood and began stalking toward him.

"Tell us everything, Hemingway. From the beginning."

"I cannot," he said, looking wildly around the room, his gaze stopping on his mother.

"That's it," she said. "I've had enough of this."

She then reached into a pocket of her gown, and Prudence knew before she finished pulling anything out just what she was doing, for she would have done the same.

She had a weapon in there. Just what, Prudence had no idea. But she didn't want to wait too long to find out.

Prudence stood as fast as she could, hoping her reflexes were quicker than Lady Hemingway's. But no sooner did Prudence have the dagger out of her pocket and behind her head did Lady Hemingway have her pistol out and cocked.

Prudence had to make a decision – did she throw it and risk killing the woman, her mother's best friend, when she didn't know for certain the extent of her involvement, or did she stop herself and risk any of her family being killed?

It wasn't a difficult decision for her to make, but the half-second it took for her to make it was too long.

For by the time her dagger was flying through the air, Lady Hemingway had seen where the threat was lurking and had pulled the trigger.

Prudence tried to move, even as she knew it was too late.

This was the end.

CHAPTER 26

*B*enedict didn't even have time to think.

The moment he realized that Prudence was in danger, he moved, flinging himself in front of her.

He grunted at the impact to his chest as he went flying backward, dimly aware that he had knocked into Prudence as he did so, hoping he hadn't hurt her.

He lay on the floor, trying to get his bearings, hearing the chaos around him but unable to do anything about it at the moment.

"Benedict!"

Prudence was kneeling over him, her hands on his face, his chest, running over his body.

"Where are you hit? Oh my— Hudson! Come quickly. Benedict, talk to me!"

She was slapping his face now in a desperate manner, and he shut his eyes to ward off her blows as he lifted his hands to grasp hers.

"Oh, you can move. Benedict, open your eyes this instant! You cannot die, I will not let you!"

He finally did as she said, opening his eyes to find her green ones staring down at him. They were full of tears which warmed his heart, for maybe she did care for him after all.

"Do stop slapping me, Prudence."

"Then why are you lying there? And where were you shot? Are you? Yes, I saw you get hit. Tell Hudson where it hurts!"

"Give a man a moment, Prudence," he said as he shifted backward so that he was sitting against the couch, noticing that Archibald and two of his men had managed to subdue Lady Hemingway and her son. Prudence's dagger was notched into the wall right next to where Lady Hemingway had been standing.

"You missed," he said, looking at Prudence with some surprise, and she sniffed in a gesture very reminiscent of her grandmother.

"I am much more accomplished in fencing than in throwing daggers," she said. "I am most proficient in close quarters."

"I see," he said, trying not to laugh, but he couldn't help his lips from curling up at the sides.

"Prudence is right, Trundelle," Lewis, the physician, interjected as he knelt beside him. "You could be suffering some after-effects of your injury. I really should tend to it. There is a hole in your jacket – over your heart."

He wrinkled his nose as he looked around Benedict, as though searching for non-existent blood.

"It's nothing," Benedict said, "though it will likely leave a bruise."

He began to unbutton his jacket then, before reaching into his waistcoat, where he lifted out the small, hard ledger book. A book that was now destroyed, because of the bullet that sat firmly in the middle of it.

Prudence fell backward onto her heels as Lewis' eyes widened.

"Well, I'll be," he said. "You are one lucky man."

"I never would have thought so in the past," Benedict said, although he was not looking at Lewis but at Prudence now, who watched him with lips slightly parted and a sheen of tears over her eyes. "But now I believe that you are right. For I *am* a lucky man. I have the fortune of being married to a woman who I might not have chosen but who turned out to be absolutely perfect for me."

He passed the book to Prudence.

"Whatever happens, whatever you decide, I have nothing more to do with this – the revenge that I sought. It has brought me nothing but grief, and a couple of wise gentlemen proved to me that I was doing nothing but hurting myself – and the woman I loved. I will explain all, but know your brother has all the evidence I was going to use against your father and your family. I no longer have any need of it."

Prudence looked over to her brother, who nodded his head.

"It's true."

"Benedict," she said, her voice just above a whisper as her lip trembled. "I do not care about any of that anymore. I thought—I thought you had died. And you had done so protecting me, after I did just what you did and threw away your words of love. It could not have been easy for you to say such things, and I did not—"

He lifted a finger and held it against her lips.

"Why do we not both agree that we could have been much better to one another and move on from here?"

She smiled a watery smile. "I would like that very much."

"Good," he said, turning so that he was kneeling in front of her, not caring that the entirety of her family – and Lord and Lady Hemingway and the magistrate – were looking on. "Prudence, will you be my wife, in truth? In a marriage in which we will love, comfort, and honor one another, through sickness and health, forsaking all others?"

Prudence grinned. "You didn't mention anything about obeying you."

He grimaced for but a moment. "I know better than to include that."

She laughed as she looped her arms around his neck and brought her forehead to his. "I would love nothing more."

"Good," he said, pressing his lips against hers, sealing their new vows with a kiss before her brother stepped forward and interjected.

"That is quite enough of that," Remington said, clearing his throat, and Prudence laughed as she and Benedict turned to see what else he had to say.

He was now turned toward Lady Hemingway, however, arms crossed as he glared down at her.

"Why?" he asked, throwing his hands out to the side. "You were part of our family, our mother's closest friend."

Benedict looked over at the dowager duchess, who was silently weeping. He was surprised at the compassion he felt for her.

"Because my son deserved the title," she sneered. "My husband was a good man, unlike Warwick, who stole all our money in some ridiculous lie. We never quite recovered, and Warwick deserved to die for his sins. It was quite simple to kill him, you know."

"But why continue to threaten us?" Remington asked. "Many men are in line for titles and wish to inherit, but it cannot always come to fruition."

"You didn't deserve it," she said, leaning toward him with her lips pulled back, and Benedict realized that at some point in time, she had become unhinged. "You left the family. You knew nothing of being a duke, nor the responsibility that comes along with that."

"I did leave the family, and I have had to live with myself for the repercussions," Remington said. "But after everything, we have been nothing but welcoming to you. To both of you."

"Still, it should have been ours," she said. "It still could, you know."

"It could," Remington agreed. "But it also could not. Now, if that will be all," he looked to the magistrate. "You can take them away."

"My son had nothing to do with it!" Lady Hemingway protested, and Remington looked toward his cousin, the man Benedict knew he had considered a friend.

"Tell us, Hemingway, the truth this time. What was your involvement?"

Lord Hemingway hung his head. "I helped my mother when she asked for it. I didn't know the full plan, and I didn't know that she'd actually killed anyone or intended to."

"But you guessed, didn't you?" Prudence asked. "How could you not, when you walked me right beneath a falling chandelier?"

"She asked me to take you there, but never told me why," Hemingway said, looking up at her with a pained expression. "That's when I knew. Before that, I just wanted to be closer to the family. I had thought I would be when I married Juliana, but—" he looked up at Prudence's sister, lifting his shoulders. "I didn't expect to be rejected."

Juliana bit her lip, and Prudence knew her sister likely felt guilt that she had no reason to.

"Were you the one who abducted Juliana?"

"I helped, but I thought it was only to have her realize that she needed to marry."

"Juliana loved another," Prudence said, knowing that he had been hurt but unable to find it in herself to feel compassion for him, not after all that these two had done to them. "We always considered you as part of the family."

"Until now," Lady Winchester said, tapping her cane on the ground. "Well, that will be our party tonight. Thank you all for coming. As the magistrate and Matthew's men take them away, why do we not go in to dinner? I'm sure you must all be famished."

She looked around at her family, who were all staring back at her with wide eyes.

"No?" she said. "Very well, more for me, then."

And with that, she sailed out of the room, apparently considering her role in this mystery complete.

Benedict looked at Prudence, and together they shared a smile that meant more to him than anything else ever could.

He had found what true happiness meant. And he would never be more grateful.

DESPITE MOST OF them losing their appetites following the scene with Lord and Lady Hemingway, the entire family, save the dowager duchess, found themselves hungry soon enough and entered the dining room for a rather subdued dinner.

Except, after a time, the air around them seemed to change, and it was Juliana who first voiced what they were all feeling.

"I know I should be upset about all that happened, but is it odd that the relief is most overwhelming?" she asked, and they all slowly began to nod.

Prudence ate distractedly, for there was still much unresolved in her life – the part of her life that included Benedict.

They had sat next to one another, and while they didn't speak directly, Prudence couldn't help but steal glances at him now and then, her face warming like an innocent young woman – which she had been not long ago, she realized – every time his eyes caught hers.

She had realized how stubborn she had been, yes, but the question was, would he allow her in, after all that had happened, or would he be afraid of losing her and use that to push her away? She didn't know – she couldn't – until they were alone together.

Instead of retiring with the ladies after dinner, Prudence placed a hand on Benedict's arm before either of them could move from the table.

"It's... it's been a long day," she said, her heart seemingly beating faster, if that were actually possible, as she looked up into his eyes. "Could we go home?"

"Home?" he repeated, hope lighting his eyes. "As in... to my – our – townhouse?"

"Yes," she said with a soft smile, and while Benedict nodded slowly as though still in disbelief, Prudence turned to the rest of her family.

"We shall be going now, but I do want to say that I am ever so grateful to have you all in my life. And Grandmother?"

Lady Winchester turned.

"I believe you are the most intelligent person I have ever met."

Lady Winchester winked at her as Prudence looped her hand through Benedict's arm and allowed him to lead her out of the house and into the carriage. But it wouldn't be until they arrived home that she would say what she wanted to say.

For this was important. A moment that she couldn't – wouldn't – blunder.

CHAPTER 27

*J*efferson didn't comment on Prudence's presence when they walked in the door, although Benedict could tell by the rising of his eyebrows that he was surprised, if nothing else.

"Lord Trundelle. Lady Trundelle," was all he said before he took their cloaks, as well as the valise that contained a few of Prudence's belongings. She had left everything else, and Benedict hadn't touched anything, preferring to walk by the closed door that was her room as though it didn't exist.

"Shall we go upstairs?" Prudence asked him, her green eyes revealing nothing, and Benedict nodded, even as his heart pounded hard in his chest. After everything he had been through, everything that he had thought mattered, he realized now that nothing would ever hold such significance as this conversation he was about to have with Prudence. For the rest of his life would all come down to this.

He followed her into her bedroom, realizing as he did so that he no longer wanted this to be her bedroom – he wanted her to share his. But first, he had to know if she still wanted to share a life with him.

"Benedict—" she began, turning to him, just as he said, "Prudence—" and they both laughed a little nervously before he took her hand and sat her down on the bed beside him.

"Are you sure you are all right, after everything that you have gone through?"

She cocked her head to the side as her mouth curled up into a small smile.

"You should know by now, Benedict, that I would not allow such a little thing as my cousin and his mother nearly murdering us to affect me, now, would I?" Her smile fell now, however, as she looked down at her hands. "It is just... I cannot seem to rid my mind of the image of that bullet hitting you. Oh, Benedict, I thought you were dead. I thought that I would have to bury you without you knowing how I truly felt, that despite what I said, I do still love you, and if anything happened to you... my heart would truly break. It is one thing to part with you, knowing you are still out there in the world, but quite another to know that you... that you would be..."

Benedict tentatively reached out and cradled her face in his hands.

"It's all right, Prudence. It didn't happen. We are not meant to part quite yet."

She took a breath, looking somewhere at the centre of his chest, which was not at all like Prudence. Then she returned her gaze to his, and Benedict vowed that he would spend the rest of his life trying to bring light and laughter to those eyes instead of any pain or sorrow.

"Are you truly committed to releasing your hate on my family? My brother? I can understand how you might never forgive my father – many people never will – but I do not think I can live with you being against the other people I love the most."

He squeezed her hands.

"I have done many wrongs in my life, Prudence, the worst of which was saying things to you that I didn't mean. Most of it I said in order to push you away, as I thought I was protecting you from being hurt even worse in the future, for what you would feel once I completed the plan I had set out. But another mistake was holding onto the pain of the past. My parents might have had their faults, as everyone does, but they were good people and they wouldn't want me to live like this."

She nodded slowly. "What about children?" she asked. "If it does not happen for us, I understand and am perfectly content with Martin's children inheriting. But... would you be open to the possibility of becoming a father?"

Benedict thought that his heart might have flipped over in his chest at her question.

"I always thought I would make the most terrible of fathers, that it would be too difficult for children to love me and for me to love them in turn," he said, hearing the gruffness in his voice. "But then, I also thought I could never be a husband, and here I am, wishing for nothing else but to spend the rest of my life with you."

She smiled then, one that reached her eyes, and Benedict breathed a sigh of relief.

"After everything I've done... will you still have me? Could you still love me?"

"Absolutely," she said, and then leaned in and sealed her promise with a kiss – one that promised a lot more to come, both tonight and far into the future.

* * *

"I THINK, Archibald, you should hire a new detective," Emma said, her lips curled up into a smile.

Matthew arched a brow from across the dinner table. "Should I now?"

"Yes," Emma said, bringing her cup to her lips. "For Lady Winchester did what you and your men never did quite accomplish – solve the case."

Matthew sighed as he looked down, causing Prudence to feel rather sorry for him, but everyone else chuckled good-naturedly until her grandmother banged her cane on the ground.

"As it happened, Mr. Archibald over there solved it around the same time as I did," she said, and Prudence knew that she wasn't lying, for her grandmother would have been pleased to take all the credit if she felt it was her due. "However, he was gracious enough to allow me the scene to have it all play out. It worked out quite well, do you not think?"

They all nodded as the first course was set in front of them. Prudence looked over at Benedict and squeezed his leg beneath the table. It was one of the first times they had both joined the entirety of her family for dinner. She knew her husband was not *completely* at ease with her family, and while he was still silent and broody, he was there.

Besides, she knew what was hiding beneath all that broodiness, waiting to emerge once they returned home.

"It is all rather sad, though, is it not?" Prudence's mother asked, and they all nodded as they considered the outcome. Lord Hemingway had been tried in the House of Lords, but had been acquitted of any murder charge, which Prudence considered was fair, for he hadn't actually killed anyone, although he very well could have. It had been a rather gripping case, being that the Duke of Warwick, the man who was originally suspected of killing his father, was on the other side.

But, at the end of it all, there was no evidence of Lord

Hemingway's wrongdoing, and his mother's letter had been the final proof needed to declare his innocence.

As for Lady Hemingway...

"I would have preferred that she had been tried," Juliana said with a sigh. "I know the outcome was the same, but she should have had to suffer some humiliation for what she did."

"Of course she should have," their grandmother said. "But look at all she did to push her son into the duke's title. She would never allow him – or the Hemingway name — to suffer through a trial."

It seemed she had availed herself of the very same poison she had used on the duke. Before she had departed the world, however, she had left a long and detailed letter outlining her actions, so that her son wouldn't be found guilty of any of them.

His only crime, it seemed, had been doing what his mother had asked of him.

"In the end, at least she did right by her son," Benedict said, surprising them all by speaking, though they all began to nod slowly at his words. "She could have left him to take the fall for it all."

"That is true," Maria said softly. "There is something to be said for that."

They were all silent for a moment as they considered the sins of the people who had been considered family.

"It's over," Giles said, circling his fingers around the glass in front of him. "I have some amends of my own to make. My father carried out a lot of misdeeds, and, with Trundelle's help, I am going to try to right some of his wrongs."

His mother began to protest, but Giles held up a hand. "It's only fair. My inheritance included ill-gotten funds and they need to go back where they belong. Trundelle himself has agreed to forgive some of the debts that were owed to him."

Benedict nodded. "It will be a case-by-case basis, but for some – such as the new Lord Dennison, who has done nothing wrong but be related to the previous one – I will make some concessions."

Giles continued. "As for the threat our family has been under... while it might not have come to an end in a manner that we would have all desired, we are still sitting here, together, alive and well – and with a few additional family members."

It was rather interesting, wasn't it, that they had all found love through such turbulent times? Perhaps it was what they needed, Prudence mused – to be shaken from the lives in which they had previously just existed, instead of actually lived.

"Has anyone been to Angelo's recently?" Giles asked now, breaking the silence once more, and Prudence choked on her wine as the rest of them shook their heads. "Heard the new sensation hasn't been around as often as he used to – the Robertson fellow."

Oh, dear. Prudence couldn't look over at Benedict, for if she did, she would likely give herself away.

Which was why she was more surprised than anyone when Benedict was the one to answer Giles.

"Perhaps he's found someone else to fence with, away from Angelo's."

They had been doing a great deal of fencing. But their fencing was best done in private, for it often led to other activities.

"Still, he was making such a name for himself," Giles said, shaking his head. "'Tis a shame that he wouldn't continue on."

"Oh, I think he will," Prudence said, unable to stop

herself. For there was one thing she was not – a quitter. "It was likely too much notoriety all at once. For he is a rather young man, is he not?"

"That's right," Giles said with a nod toward them. "I heard that you faced him a time or two, Trundelle."

Benedict nodded quickly before hiding his face behind his cup.

"What's he like?" Giles pressed, obviously not recognizing that Benedict had no wish to continue on the topic.

Benedict cleared his throat, keeping his eyes clear of Prudence.

"He is... very skilled, that is for certain. He has had training from Angelo, but from another source as well, someone who taught him to be edgier, more cunning. He has very quick reflexes and seems to know what his opponent is going to do before he even knows it himself."

Giles nodded, looking impressed.

"Well, I hope to meet him myself one day."

"Oh, I'm sure you will, Giles," Prudence said slowly. "I'm sure you will."

Giles narrowed his eyes at her. "You know something."

"Know what?" Prudence asked, feigning innocence.

"Something about this Robertson. Were you there for his second match against Trundelle?"

"Yes." Prudence nodded. "I was there."

"And?"

"And... it is like Benedict said. The man is very accomplished."

Prudence heard a gasp from across the table, and she could tell from Juliana's wide eyes and hand over her mouth that she had determined just who Mr. Peter Robertson was. It shouldn't have been overly difficult, for all in the family knew of Prudence's love of fencing. They likely just didn't realize the extent to which she would go to continue her skills.

"Oh, for goodness' sake, Giles, take your head out of your ass and realize that she *is* Peter Robertson," Lady Winchester finally said, banging her spoon this time instead of her cane. Giles whipped his head around toward Prudence as Prudence glared at her grandmother.

"What does it matter?" her grandmother asked with a shrug. "It is not as though your brother can lock you in the house any longer, and your husband already knows."

Giles was gaping at her open-mouthed. "Is this true?" he finally managed, to which Prudence nodded firmly.

"Yes."

He turned his gaze to Benedict. "And you knew?"

"After a time," Benedict said, and Prudence could tell he didn't want to get caught in the middle of the argument that was sure to come.

"Good heavens," Prudence's mother said, and it was a wonder she didn't start crossing herself.

"But how—" Giles began, but then interrupted himself. "Conway."

"I shall neither confirm nor deny Hugo's involvement in my plans," Prudence said, holding her chin high, refusing to be shamed about one of the things she loved most in her life.

Giles shook his head. "I don't blame you."

"Pardon me?" It was Prudence's turn to be shocked.

"You always were one of the best fencers I have ever known. It was a pity you couldn't compete. If this allows you to do so, then – with Trundelle's blessing, of course – so be it."

"Giles, you know far better than that," Emma said with a cheeky smile for her husband. "There is no *allowing* here. Only accepting."

"Very well," Giles said with a chuckle. "Actually, Prudence, I am proud of you."

Now *that* caught her off-guard.

"You are?"

"I am. Now, unless anyone else has anymore surprises for the night..." He looked around the table and they all shook their heads. "Let's eat."

It wasn't until they arrived home a few hours later that Benedict squeezed Prudence's hand and pulled her close.

"I know it is the middle of the night, but you have me craving a fencing match," he said, and she could feel the smile in his voice. "What do you say we have a round or two?"

"I say," she said, turning toward him and wrapping her arms around his neck as he lifted her up higher, "that is the best idea you could present."

And, after greeting Angus, the dog who Benedict had been reluctant to own but quickly embraced, they began in the fencing room – although that wasn't where they finished.

EPILOGUE

ONE YEAR LATER

"*Must* we really attend?" Benedict asked as they walked up the front steps of Warwick House. He was never particularly comfortable at the mansion, but he had become more used to it over the past year that he and Prudence had been married.

His brother had also encouraged him to come, although he couldn't forget the last ball he had attended, when Prudence had nearly been crushed by a chandelier.

But everything had changed since then. He and Prudence were happy, and the Remington family was no longer under threat. He supposed that meant he should simply enjoy himself, but he still wasn't exactly that man.

"There is no other social event I would ask you to attend but this one," Prudence said, lacing her arm through his as they continued through the foyer, where Emma and Giles were greeting their guests. "This ball has become a tradition of sorts, for it was where Emma and Giles discovered they loved one another. Besides, if we get bored, we can always find my old fencing room," she said, winking at him suggestively, and he couldn't help but chuckle.

They greeted Giles and Emma before continuing on to the main room, where Benedict's brother, Martin, and his wife, Amelia, quickly found them.

"Prudence, you work miracles," Martin said, and Prudence cocked an eyebrow at him in question of his words.

"You have convinced Benedict to attend a ball, for no reason other than he actually wanted to attend. How did you do it?"

"I asked," Prudence said.

"She was… quite convincing," he was compelled to add, causing Amelia to cough as their Aunt Emily joined them.

"Benedict. Prudence. It is lovely to see you," she said, "especially at such an event. It is hard to believe that the result of your beginnings has ended so well."

"Yes," Prudence said. "Our beginning and the following tumultuous times."

The musicians started to play, and Martin led Amelia out onto the dance floor. Emma, Juliana, and Maria walked over to Prudence, and Benedict took a step backward to give them some space.

"This is where it all began," came a voice in Benedict's ear, and he turned to find Giles standing there, a wistful look on his face. "Emma was standing there with my sisters, watching me dance by her. The look on her face… I didn't understand it at the time. And my grandmother was there, watching with them. I wonder if she knew."

"I wouldn't put it past her," Benedict said wryly as Archibald and Lewis joined them. This was also the only *ton* event the two men would ever attend, for they wouldn't otherwise receive an invitation or have any desire to go.

Giles chuckled as he shook his head. "I barely knew my sisters then, having just returned home. Had no idea I even had a brother. Possessed no inkling that I would need to hire a detective. And never had reason to believe I would ever meet the reclusive Lord Trundelle."

He tipped his glass toward them. "How things have changed. And I couldn't be happier about it." He was silent for a moment before he continued. "Well, then, I must go and collect my bride. We have a date on a balcony."

Before he could explain what he meant by that, he was off, leaving the three of them.

"I have a patient to see to, in a very private parlor," Lewis said with a twinkle in his eye before he went to find Maria, which led Archibald to look at Benedict and say, "and I've a mystery to go solve. One that I will likely spend the rest of my life attempting to figure out."

Benedict paused for a moment before walking over to Prudence, who had been left alone, watching the dance floor. He held out his hand.

"A dance, my lady?"

She looked up at him with surprise in her wide, green eyes.

"You don't dance."

"I didn't," he corrected. "But there are many things I didn't used to do. And I do dance – with the correct partner."

Her lips curled into the smile he loved so much.

"Very well, then," she said as he led her out onto the floor.

Prudence melted into his arms, and Benedict held her closer than he knew was proper, but he didn't care – for what would the consequence be? That they created a scandal? That he had to marry her? Nothing of the sort mattered to him anymore, as long as Prudence loved him.

"No one ever used to ask me to dance," she said,

surprising him, and he leaned back slightly away from her so that he could look into her eyes.

"That cannot be true," he said more vehemently than he meant to.

"It is," she said with a shrug. "Juliana always said that I was too intimidating to men, and she was likely right. My mother always told me to be more like Maria. But when Giles decided to marry Emma instead of the woman all felt was perfect, I realized that I shouldn't change myself to become someone I thought other people might like."

Benedict squeezed her closer. "I am very glad you didn't. For there is no one else like you, Prudence, and I couldn't live without you in my life."

She tilted her head up toward him. "Have I told you how much I love you?"

"I still do not believe it, so I suppose you must continue to do so."

She nodded. "I will. And—" Her voice caught. "Someone else is going to love you very soon, too."

Benedict looked down sharply at her, wondering whatever she could mean. "You are all I— oh. *Oh*."

Her expression was flitting between excitement and worry, and Benedict wanted nothing more than for her to allow herself to feel what she was feeling.

"I am happy, Prudence."

"You are?'

"I am," he said with a nod. "I can do anything, if I have you."

"And I you," she said, leaning up and kissing him on the lips despite the gasps from those close to them or the circle that seemed to grow quickly around them.

Prudence tugged Benedict away to the side of the dance floor.

"I always wondered what my life would look like," she

said softly, reaching out to intertwine their fingers. "Now? Mystery solved."

"Mystery solved," he agreed. "And a very fine ending it is."

THE END

* * *

DEAR READER,

HERE WE ARE, at the end of the series! I hope you enjoyed Prudence and Benedict's story as well as the conclusion to the mystery that the Remington family has been attempting to solve since we first met them in The Mystery of the Debonair Duke. I loved writing this family, who at some point in the story, took over and seemed to write the books themselves!

I appreciate all of you who have kept with or followed the series from book to book, eager to discover just who was behind the threat to the family.

As sad as I am to leave the Remingtons, I hope you join me in the next journey. The Reckless Rogues series tells the story of a book club of ladies who are not exactly into conventional stories, and a thrill-seeking group of gentlemen looking for adventure beyond their everyday responsibilities. When they each find a riddle leading to treasure, their focus changes — and they are surprised when love finds them along the way. The first book, The Earl's Secret, is a brother's-best-friend, second chance romance featuring a plucky heroine who trouble follows around, and a charming earl who has never quite gotten over her. I have a preview to share with you on the following pages, or find it on Amazon here.

I'm also thrilled to be part of an anthology including 19 brand new stories from some of your favourite historical romance authors! You can preorder I Like Big Dukes and I Cannot Lie, which will be released September 12th, for only 99 cents.

And if you haven't yet signed up for my newsletter, I would love to have you join! You will receive Unmasking a Duke for free, as well as links to giveaways, sales, new releases, and stories about my coffee addiction, my struggle to keep my plants alive, and how much trouble one loveable wolf-looka-like dog can get into.

www.elliestclair.com/ellies-newsletter

Or you can join my Facebook group, Ellie St. Clair's Ever Afters, and stay in touch daily.

With love,
Ellie

The Earl's Secret
Reckless Rogues Book 1

Thrust together in search of a treasure, Cassandra and Devon must decide if they will take a second chance at love...

Five years ago, Lady Cassandra was left heartbroken, ruined, and regretful. Since the night her brother's best friend left her to face the consequences of their forbidden liaison alone, the only love she will accept is in the pages of the scandalous romance novels she and her closest friends read in secret.

Devon Addison, Earl of Covington, has given up hope in finding love again. He finds his thrills in wagers and adventures proposed by the equally bored lords and second sons of his circle, intent on forgetting the sister of his best friend.

When the lords and ladies stumble upon a riddle that promises to lead to treasure, they each resolve to find it first. When Cassandra and Devon find themselves searching together, however, will they find a completely unexpected prize instead?

The first book of the Reckless Rogues series is a brother's-best-friend, second chance steamy regency romance featuring a plucky heroine who trouble follows around, and a charming earl who has never quite gotten over her.

THE EARL'S SECRET -
CHAPTER ONE

"*I*t is not a true romance if it does not have a happy ending."

"It is not a true romance if it does not have a happy ending."

Cassandra's bold statement was met with the expected chorus of opinions. In a room of women who all passionately preferred their own brand of romance and never hesitated to share their true thoughts, her view would not go unchallenged.

But she maintained her position as she sat in the center of the room and placed her hand over her heart as though making a lifelong vow.

Although she supposed in a way, she was.

"Why did we just put ourselves through such tragedy for entertainment?" she continued, her spine straight in her perch on the middle cushion of the crimson French sofa, which was beginning to show all if its decades. "I apologize, Faith, for I know the book was your choice, but I was so *invested* in their love, and then for it all to end in such a tortuous manner... I simply cannot go through that again."

"Cassandra," Faith said, tilting her head at her. "You are being overly dramatic. It is still a romance because they fell in love. Yes, they allowed external forces to come between them, but that does not mean the story is not worth reading. Did we not learn something from it?"

"Yes," Cassandra said with a firm nod of her head. "Never trust a gentleman who is more in love with a ghost that his wife."

Persephone, who they affectionately called Percy, started to snicker at that, while Faith rolled her eyes. Faith's sister, Hope, sighed herself, and Cassandra knew that she likely agreed with her. The fair-haired, blue-eyed Hope lived up to her name, always seeing the best in everyone around her, while Faith was far more suspicious of anyone who entered her life.

One could tell their personalities by their choice in books – which made Cassandra all the more worried about what Madeline might pick the following week.

Percy held up a hand before they could begin arguing again.

"Before we delve deeper into this conversation, perhaps we should pour ourselves a drink."

"An excellent idea," Cassandra said, smiling wickedly as she walked to the sideboard, where her brother, Gideon, kept his alcohol. She had a feeling he knew that she and her friends often helped themselves, but they each took a turn providing sustenance for their meetings so that there was never enough missing for him to have reason to accuse them.

She reached underneath and found five short glasses, lining them up in a row on the chipped wood of the sideboard above. She generously poured each one, and then served them to her friends before sitting back in her own place on the sofa, closing her eyes and taking a deep sip, welcoming the fiery warmth as it slid down her throat – just as the door opened, startling all of them.

"Gideon, I—oh, excuse me."

The deep, bass voice echoed through the room and straight into Cassandra's soul. It was a voice she knew well, one that she usually attempted to avoid.

For it brought nothing but trouble.

She shot to her feet so quickly that the remnants of her drink spilled out and splashed over her dress, but she disregarded that as she locked eyes with the dark, unreadable ones of the man in front of her – the man she had allowed to get under her skin, not to mention a few other places he should never have been – once too many times.

His broad, full lips curled into a smirk as his eyes wandered from her face down the entirety of her body to the kid slippers that covered her toes and back up again. His scrutiny was more fiery than the liquid that was dripping over her and she shivered from the intensity of it.

"Having ourselves a good time, are we ladies?" he asked, although he kept his eyes on Cassandra.

"We are having a private meeting," she said, straightening her shoulders and meeting his gaze full-on, refusing to cow before him. "One to which gentlemen are not invited. I believe Gideon is hosting a gathering of his own – one that you *are* likely welcome at – in the drawing room. This is the parlor."

"So it would seem," he said, his eyes sweeping around the room, missing nothing, including the books that each of them held in their laps. Cassandra gripped hers tightly in her hand as she moved it slightly behind her back so that he wouldn't comment upon it. She had nothing to fear from the man, she reminded herself. The worst he could do was tell Gideon what they were doing in here, and the truth was, she didn't think her brother would overly care.

"Lord Covington," Hope said belatedly, standing with a slight bow, one which they all followed – even Cassandra, as much as it aggravated her to do so.

She could tell he was completely aware of her feelings as his grin stretched wider and his eyes turned darker.

"Lady Cassandra," he said, slipping his hand into his jacket and producing his handkerchief with a flourish, "I believe you might be in need of this."

Cassandra's hands balled into fists as she wanted to deny it – deny *him* – with everything within her. But she could feel the close gaze of her friends and she knew that she was best to simply take it from him and then hope he would leave.

"Thank you," she said through gritted teeth, crossing the room toward him and practically ripping it from his fingers before lifting it up to her body. Then she realized that two could play this game.

Ensuring that no one else in the room – except Lord Covington or Devon as she had always known him – could see her actions, she smiled coyly as she brought the handkerchief to her neck, slowly wiping away drops of the drink from her collarbones and then down to her cleavage. She dipped his handkerchief, noting it was embroidered with his initials, D.A., into the valley of her breasts, watching his nostrils flare as she did so.

She fixed an innocent look upon her face as she lifted the handkerchief and held it out toward him.

"Thank you," she said, annoyed by the breathy tone of her voice as she realized that her plan had unintended consequences when warmth washed over her, her teasing affecting her as much as she had meant to affect him.

His ungloved hands brushed against hers when he accepted it back, causing a most unwelcome tingle to rush up her arms and down her spine. He crushed the handkerchief in his hand as he nodded to her and then the rest of her friends before he turned on his heel and swiftly left the room.

Leaving quite the shocked air behind him.

Cassandra's shoulders stiffened for a moment, knowing what she would be facing when she turned around to her friends.

"Well," Percy said with wide eyes. "That was... interesting."

Madeline, the only one of the women who knew the full story of Cassandra's history with the earl, was wearing a knowing smile as she crossed her arms over her chest, waiting for Cassandra's response. Some help she was.

Cassandra cleared her throat.

"Shall we return to our discussion?"

Faith lifted a brow.

"Perhaps you should first tell us of what just transpired between you and the earl."

Cassandra should have expected this, although she wasn't entirely sure how to explain. Behind closed doors here in their book club room they were not the most proper of women, but they were still, for the most part, innocent young ladies who would be rather shocked if they knew the full truth.

"Lord Covington is my brother's closest friend," she said, lifting a hand as though it didn't mean anything.

"Of that we are aware," Faith said. "But I can hardly see how him being the friend of your brother could lead to such... tension."

Cassandra walked over to the sideboard and repoured her brandy before taking her seat, giving herself a moment to collect her thoughts by sipping from her glass.

He and my brother spent much of their youth torturing me," she said, hoping her tone was nonchalant. "I have never been particularly pleased with the part he played in encouraging Gideon."

"How long did this *teasing* last?" Percy asked, clearly understanding there was, perhaps, more to the story.

"It has never ended," Cassandra said, allowing her ire at the man to flow into her words. "Although I haven't seem him in some time. I have tended to avoid him since I... returned."

"Sometimes they say teasing is a form of flirtation," Hope said in her soft voice. "He could have a particular penchant for you."

"That is a lovely way to look at it, Hope, but I can assure you that he most certainly does not."

Hope shrugged as she took a small sip of her drink. Cassandra knew Hope would never admit to another soul outside of this room that she enjoyed it, preferring her lemonades when drinking in public. But then, she was as sweet of a woman as one could ever find and would never want to disturb her mother nor cause any discord.

"Lord Covington is nothing more than a nuisance, and a nuisance that I would prefer to avoid," Cassandra said, picking up her book to note to the rest of them that she was finished with their current conversation. "Now, can we discuss how much better this book would have been had the hero not been killed in the end?"

They seemed to accept her explanation – or at least respect her obvious preference to not to discuss it any further – for now, at least. It wasn't until the women had concluded their book discussion for the day and departed, leaving only Madeline and Cassandra, that Cassandra knew she would have to face the truth.

"So tell me," Madeline said, as she settled back against the sofa, her brown eyes flashing in amusement as she looked at Cassandra impishly, "just what are you going to do about Lord Covington?"

"There is nothing to *do* about him," Cassandra said, walking around the room and collecting their glasses. Of course the maids would be in to clean, but Cassandra didn't want them knowing exactly what she and her friends were doing in here. It was one thing to discuss books that none of them were supposed to be reading, and quite something else for them to be drinking brandy while doing so.

Her mother was aware of their book club, but as far as she knew, they were reading *An Enquiry Into the Duties of the Female Sex* and discussing just how they should be conducting themselves in order to attract proper husbands.

"Cassandra, the moment he stepped into the room, the air was filled with an obvious edge between the two of you. Perhaps what was between you was never completely resolved."

"It *was*," Cassandra said with vehemence in her voice, more so to convince herself than Madeline. "It was a mistake. One that should never have happened."

"And left you ruined."

"No one knows that."

"Except you. And him."

"What does it matter?" Cassandra asked, lifting her hands. "Only my mother and Gideon were aware of my immoral choice, and they ensured I paid for it. No one else knows anything for certain, so therefore, is no slight on my honor."

"The man you marry might find out."

"It would be too late by then," Cassandra said through gritted teeth, for it was a battle that she had fought within herself for far too long.

For it was the very thing that had held her back from marriage – the knowledge that she would have to hide the truth from her husband until her marriage night, and once he found out, there was no consequence that could turn out in her favor.

It was hardly a way to start a marriage, and for that reason, she had resisted for far too long. Of course, it had been rather difficult to explain to her mother just exactly *why* she had refused any suitor who showed interest in her.

She was the daughter of a duke, the sister of an earl who would one day be one of the most powerful men in the country. And here she was, avoiding any gentleman interested in her.

"There is one other thing you are forgetting," Madeline said, lifting one of her dark eyebrows, with that expression that terrified most men, intimidating them from coming too close.

"Which is?"

"That you cannot help yourself from being attracted to him, that no other man has ever been good enough for you."

"That's not true," Cassandra said staunchly.

"It is," Madeline said, though her voice held nonchalance as though she had no desire to argue with Cassandra about it. "I don't understand why the two of you did not just marry and be done with it."

"Because we can hardly stand in the same room together, let alone in front of an altar," Cassandra said. The truth was, she had hardly spoken to Devon after... it... happened, that she refused to allow him close to her once more. "And I could never trust him again," she finished softly.

She had told herself to move on, had assumed that she would in due time – that soon enough, another man would enter her life, one who was appropriate, who she could tolerate, who would be her friend and her husband.

But no other stirred her soul. Not like Lord Covington had, even if it was not always in the way she would prefer.

She just had no idea what she was supposed to do about it.

* * *

You can soon find The Earl's Secret on Amazon and in Kindle Unlimited!

ALSO BY ELLIE ST. CLAIR

Reckless Rogues
The Earls's Secret
Prequel, The Duke's Treasure, available in:
I Like Big Dukes and I Cannot Lie

The Remingtons of the Regency
The Mystery of the Debonair Duke
The Secret of the Dashing Detective
The Clue of the Brilliant Bastard
The Quest of the Reclusive Rogue

To the Time of the Highlanders
A Time to Wed
A Time to Love
A Time to Dream

Thieves of Desire
The Art of Stealing a Duke's Heart
A Jewel for the Taking
A Prize Worth Fighting For
Gambling for the Lost Lord's Love
Romance of a Robbery

The Bluestocking Scandals
Designs on a Duke
Inventing the Viscount

Discovering the Baron

The Valet Experiment

Writing the Rake

Risking the Detective

A Noble Excavation

A Gentleman of Mystery

The Bluestocking Scandals Box Set: Books 1-4

The Bluestocking Scandals Box Set: Books 5-8

Blooming Brides

A Duke for Daisy

A Marquess for Marigold

An Earl for Iris

A Viscount for Violet

The Blooming Brides Box Set: Books 1-4

Happily Ever After

The Duke She Wished For

Someday Her Duke Will Come

Once Upon a Duke's Dream

He's a Duke, But I Love Him

Loved by the Viscount

Because the Earl Loved Me

Happily Ever After Box Set Books 1-3

Happily Ever After Box Set Books 4-6

The Victorian Highlanders

Duncan's Christmas - (prequel)

Callum's Vow

Finlay's Duty

Adam's Call

Roderick's Purpose

Peggy's Love

The Victorian Highlanders Box Set Books 1-5

Searching Hearts

Duke of Christmas (prequel)

Quest of Honor

Clue of Affection

Hearts of Trust

Hope of Romance

Promise of Redemption

Searching Hearts Box Set (Books 1-5)

Standalones

Always Your Love

The Stormswept Stowaway

A Touch of Temptation

Christmastide with His Countess

Her Christmas Wish

Merry Misrule

A Match Made at Christmas

For a full list of all of Ellie's books, please see

www.elliestclair.com/books.

ABOUT THE AUTHOR

Ellie has always loved reading, writing, and history. For many years she has written short stories, non-fiction, and has worked on her true love and passion -- romance novels.

In every era there is the chance for romance, and Ellie enjoys exploring many different time periods, cultures, and geographic locations. No matter when or where, love can always prevail. She has a particular soft spot for the bad boys of history, and loves a strong heroine in her stories.

Ellie and her husband love nothing more than spending time at home with their children and Husky cross. Ellie can typically be found at the lake in the summer, pushing the stroller all year round, and, of course, with her computer in her lap or a book in hand.

She also loves corresponding with readers, so be sure to contact her!

www.elliestclair.com
ellie@elliestclair.com

Ellie St. Clair's Ever Afters Facebook Group

Printed by Amazon Italia Logistica S.r.l.
Torrazza Piemonte (TO), Italy

55289286R00143